THE
Voices
OF
Gable

To Sergio —
Thank You!
Enjoy the read —
Christ's blessings
Robbie Lamberson

ROBBIE LAMBERSON

ISBN 978-1-64114-869-6 (Paperback)
ISBN 978-1-64114-870-2 (Digital)

Christian Faith Publishing, Inc.
296 Chestnut Street
Meadville, PA 16335
www.christianfaithpublishing.com

Printed in the United States of America

Acknowledgment

This is the second manuscript that Linda Marler, my friend and advisor, has edited and proofread before it was presented to my publisher. I am extremely grateful for her effort and her encouragement.

A fourth novel is now in the works so don't go too far my sweet friend. I will once again have need of your talent.

Prologue

The book lay open before them. The book was always open and had remained open for the last seven thousand earth years.

Name after name after name had been added since the first two were written down soon after the enemy had been given his temporary dominion. Each name had a history. Each name had a story. Each name was unique. Each name had one thing, and one thing only, in common.

The Master turned the last page. Both their eyes were fixed on Him. They had known this moment was coming, but neither knew the day or the hour.

"Michael!"

Michael had served All Mighty God as the archangel since before time began; the leader of all the Master's angels. Michael had always devoted his every moment to his Omnipresent God, and always would, of that there was no question. When the Master spoke, Michael never failed to have the same feeling—a feeling somewhere between awe, excitement, undying love, a tinge of fear, and complete utter devotion. The Master's voice was unlike any other sound in the heavenly realm. It had power that was unmatchable and at times frightening; a strength that was beyond description but held a love that Michael could feel deep in his spirit. The Heavenly Father's voice filled every void. It came from nowhere and everywhere.

Standing before them, Michael immediately replied, "Yes, Yahweh?"

"It is time."

There was no need for Him to say more. All Michael needed to know were in the three words the Master had spoken. He had been waiting for this moment for a long time; all of heaven had been waiting on this moment.

Michael had been in countless wars over the eons of time, wars fought against the enemy's legions, the legions intent on destroying God's creation, led by a mighty warrior, Lucifer, who once served alongside Michael. Lucifer's warriors were powerful, that was true. They had authority over God's favored creation that lived on the small planet He created for them. Therefore, they did have a tactical advantage when fighting battles there. And this is where Michael had been instructed by Almighty God to conduct an epic battle.

But while the enemy was dependent solely on deception, Michael and his warrior angels served the Master. The spirit of Elohim was above any other might or power; there was no one or nothing to compare to Him. He had no equal. Michael and his army were swept into victorious battles by His Spirit.

Michael went to his post and summoned his four chief angels, the most trusted of all his commanders—Barael, Aaron, Orion, and Hebron.

They arrived immediately, each with a mix of excitement and trepidation. Each of these mighty angels was completely faithful to the Master, which by extension meant they were completely faithful to Michael. His orders came directly from Elohim and were obeyed without question or hesitation.

The four had fought alongside and behind Michael for eons in spiritual warfare encompassing countless battles. The four were supremely confident in the powers that came from their Lord, but they never underestimated the enemy for to do so could mean the difference in a soul. And the angels knew there was nothing more important to the Master than the souls of His children; even the loss of a single soul so grieved Him. And as He grieved, so grieved they. These four, the most powerful and loyal angels, would do anything to prevent that grief, including laying down their lives without hesitancy.

They stood in silent anticipation for whatever mighty effort was required of them and ready to call to arms their own legions of angels that were numbered in the countless thousands.

Michael gave each of them their task; each was given succinct, complete directives with all they required in order to carry it out. Michael's orders were always so. Each stood stoically for a count; it was not lost on Michael. Neither was it lost on the Master.

As one their enormous wings spread out from their massive backs and they were gone.

The end had begun.

PART 1

1865

1

I try not to let it overtake me, but my heart is heavy and my soul weeps. How long will I be banished to this place? After all it wasn't me who was the guilty one, it was done to me. I was the victim and yet the evil ones are free.

I walk these paths day after day and night after night. I'm not allowed to leave the grounds. I don't know how I know this, but it is a rule that is branded upon me, and beyond doubt, I cannot step outside.

There are others here. I can't see them, but I feel their presence. Like me, they are waiting… but for what? Rescue perhaps? But where are we supposed to be? Where do we belong now that we are dead?

I clearly see the times of my life, when I was alive and could feel the wind in my hair and the warmth of the sun on my skin. I vividly recall the way my heart would flutter in my breast when he came into a room. The color of his eyes as he lay beside me and the deep pit of grief I spiraled into when he left me. But I mustn't dwell on his memory any longer. It brings the sadness back like a crescendo, and I have been over it more times than I can count over these years.

Today is a beautiful spring day. Standing in the midst of the monuments, with the names of those who have been laid to rest here engraved on their marble countenances. I can hear the rustle of the blackjack trees as the dead leaves fall to make room for the buds that will soon fill the trees again.

Strange, that I am allowed to hear the sounds around me. When another body is brought into these grounds, followed by grieving loved ones, I hear their sobs and their words. Some are relieved and there are no tears. These arouse my curiosity something fierce. How can this be? Invariably, when I examine the dates, after the mourners are gone, I find the deceased to have been elderly, lived a rich full life; this is attested to by the number of children and grandchildren surrounding their interment. I surmise that some illness must have caused them great pain and that is why their loved ones feel such relief that their suffering is finally over.

I felt no such relief! Abram's suffering was over, but mine began in that moment in time. And he did suffer, oh, how he suffered. Nothing I did could erase his terrible memories or silence the night-mares that were constantly with him. It is not right, not fair, for a man to endure such torture. He was weak. Even though he sur-vived with great courage, it left him weak, unable to withstand his memories.

I am grateful for this gift of hearing, and oftentimes, I believe I can smell the scent of the roses planted along the north side of the rock fence that surrounds the grounds on three sides. In late fall, when the leaves are dropping, I sometimes get the faint smell of pine cones that fall from the stately loblolly pines scattered throughout the woods.

I wonder how long I have been here. It must be many ages, as the clothes and the strange objects that bring the living and the dead to this place are unlike anything I had seen when I was alive. I am aware of the changing seasons, but I have lost count of the vast num-ber that has occurred.

There are many strange things here. Strange that my dress shows no wear after all these years. And my shoes, the dress shoes I was wearing on that day, show no signs of the countless miles I have walked within these boundaries. And no tears! I don't know what to think of that. When I lived, they fell from my eyes without ceasing. But here, though the sadness is as acute as in the beginning, there are no tears that fall and wet my face.

It was late afternoon the first time I saw him. I had finished the last day of the school year, and my students were long gone from the small school house located at the outer edge of town. I walked home the two and a half miles as I had for the last five years. I was destined to be a teacher. That's what women of my age, who are without husband or children, must do. My life was devoid of any great happiness, but I was somewhat contented with my daily rituals. My house, and it was mine now that mother and father were buried side by side here in Gable Cemetery, was my refuge; the only place I belonged.

I sat on the front porch to rest a few minutes before starting my supper and feeding the animals who even now were fussing for their meal of the day. Something caught my eye as I slowly rocked in my mother's chair. Standing up, I stared at the apparition that swerved from one side of the road to the other. Shading my eyes from the setting sun, I squinted to bring it into focus. I watched, fascinated, as it moved closer.

Just as I realized it was a man, he fell facedown in the middle of the road. I glanced frantically around as if someone might materialize and tell me what I should do. I opened the gate but stayed inside the safety of the fenced yard, hoping he would rise up and go about his business. I hated anything out of the ordinary, anything that required me to do what made me uncomfortable. But the man had not moved, and knowing my father would be furious if I refused to act in a Christian manner, I cautiously started toward the body lying on the road.

Hesitantly, at first, I made my way slowly toward the figure, which had not moved. I crept upon the strange man and stood over him, deciding he must have died here in the middle of the road. Hoping someone would come riding past and take this predicament off my hands, I glanced first left and then right, but the road remained empty. Kneeling down to look closer at the still form, I was startled to hear a whispering gasp escaping from his lips. Saliva trickling from one corner of his mouth found its way down to the dry earth and soaked into the dirt leaving a damp circle.

He looked as if he was a skeleton, as if all the meat on his bones had been used up and the carcass stubbornly refused to stop breath-

13

ing. "Mister, uh, mister!" I said loudly hoping to get a response, but it was no use. Not knowing what else to do, I ran back to the house and got a quilt off the bed in the small bedroom, wishing I had time to chase down the horse in the pasture but afraid to leave the stranger lying in the road any longer. Running back, I spread the quilt alongside of him and rolled him over onto it. It was not a struggle; he weighed no more than one of my young students. And he was still unconscious so if I added to his pain, he was blissfully unaware of it.

Dragging him toward the house was harder than I expected and took longer than I intended. Not knowing what else to do, I dragged him up the steps and over the threshold into the house before I collapsed onto the nearest chair and gasping for air, pushed my straggling hair out of my vision. Looking down at the man, I studied his face but it was impossible to guess his age; somewhere between his twenties and fifty, I surmised. But I couldn't leave him in the middle of the parlor floor, so taking a deep breath, I picked up the corners of the quilt again and pulled him into my bedroom, which was the nearest place to settle him. I somehow managed to wrestle him onto the bed before sitting down again. He still had not made a sound or awakened from his deep unconsciousness.

I was appalled at the condition of his clothes. They must have belonged to a much larger man, as they hung so loosely on him; it had to have been a struggle to keep them on his body. His shoes barely covered the top of his feet, and the soles were mostly gone. The stench that rose to my nostrils was sickening, which overcame my modesty, and without stopping to consider I had never seen a naked man before, I quickly stripped the clothes from his frail body. The shock of seeing a human body so emancipated tugged at my compassion as never before. Gathering up the putrid bundle, I threw it into a pile out the back door and going to the kitchen pumped water to be heated on the stove. There was already wood left in the cast iron cook stove from this morning. I lit a bit of kindling and blew on it to get it going and running back to check on him found him unmoved.

As the water heated, I got the pitcher, bowl, and a bar of new soap that one of my students had given me last Christmas. Believing the sweet smell of lavender might help to erase the terrible odor from him, I carried it all into the bedroom and began to wash the grime and blood from his flesh. As the layers of filth came off his body, the story of his condition was evident. Almost every inch of him was covered with scars. There were long scars that looked like they had been there for some time. Whoever sewed him up must have been blind for these scars would forever be as gruesome as they are today. His chest and his buttocks had so many burn marks I couldn't imagine having survived such torture.

Tears began to flow from my eyes. The warmth of them trailed down my cheeks and dripped from my chin, which astonished me as I could not remember the last time I had cried. I hesitated for only a moment when it came to the private parts of his body, but it was like washing a child and my embarrassment vanished immediately. It was a long and tedious process as I tried to be as gentle as I could. *Good god, who could have done this to another human being?* The question echoed through my mind.

Finishing as quickly as I could, I threw the filthy water out the back door and burned the clothing on the ground where it laid. I put smoked beef bones on the stove to make a broth and added vegetables for more flavor. I went back and forth to check on my patient, for this is how I thought of the man lying in my bed. After finishing the broth, I let it cool a bit and then carried a small bowl into the bedroom. Adding more pillows, I propped him up so he would not choke. Bit by bit, I forced a few spoonfuls into his mouth and was encouraged that he was able to swallow. Afraid he would become sick if he got too much, I decided to space out his feedings to only small amounts every few hours.

Throughout the night, I held vigil over him and as the hours passed, my curiosity grew. There was no identification in his clothing and not a cent had I found on his person. How did he survive and where was he going? For that matter, who was he? By morning, he had soiled the bedding, which I knew was a good sign. At least his innards were capable of working, but he was still deeply unconscious and unaware of his surroundings. This became a ritual over the next two days, but he was consuming more of the rich broth each time.

I tried offering up prayers for his healing. But my faith had become nonexistent over the last few years. Father had more than enough faith for both of us. He was a minister and had come to this small town in Indian Territory, formed his church, and was thrilled to watch it grow each year as he preached the word from the Holy Bible. Mother was an excellent pastor's wife—quiet, submissive, and as devout as Father. They had been married almost twenty years and had given up on having children when I miraculously came along. Mother once told me, "I know how Sarah felt when she discovered to be with child at such an old age."

I was always quite different, quiet, and obeying from the beginning, unlike most children. I preferred playing alone and seldom said a word or requested much for myself. They had produced the perfect child for themselves. I even looked like them, with mousy brown hair and hazel eyes, which were somewhat weak, and set too far apart. I was not tall, but I was not short. I was not heavy, but neither was I skinny. I was… me. Looking in the mirror, I was never under the impression that I had any claim to beauty, so therefore I never tried to improve on my looks. I was content to live my life each day as long as nothing interrupted the rituals that made our lives ordinary. Father crossed over into healing other people's battles in his congregation or refereeing church squabbles, but they did not affect our home life.

But when mother came down with the fever, all the prayers sent up to heaven were ignored by this God my father swore by, and before she stopped breathing, he came down with the same malady. I tried my best to save them. Members of the congregation came and prayed over them as I stood aside not taking part in their prayers. Somehow I had lost all of what little faith I had acquired when first accepting Jesus as my Lord and Savior. It all seemed so distant, too far away to do us any good.

They died within twenty-four hours of each other. The community came and did their duty. A pastor from the only other church in town said words over them as we buried them side by side in the small cemetery named Gable after the family who had donated a part of their land for this purpose. I shed no tears through the thin black veil attached to my black bonnet. And walking away from the crowd of Jesus worshippers, I went home and closed the door. I preferred not to have visitors, and after a few awkward visits, people honored my wishes and I was left alone. Until the man in the road interrupted.

I was getting used to caring for "the man" as I would have an abandoned kitten, or wounded bird, until the third night he had been with me. The screams that awakened me were the most terrifying sounds I had ever heard. They jolted me from a dreamless sleep, and for some moments, I was too afraid to move. Finally, realizing the horrific noises were coming from my bedroom, I grabbed my night coat and wrapping it around me, rushed to his room, carrying a coal oil lamp to see by. I was staggered at the scene before me. He was sitting up in the bed with his head thrown back, his mouth opened wide, and the horrible sounds were erupting from inside the very depths of him. His eyes protruded from their sockets and darted back and forth as if hunting for whatever monsters terrified him so. It was obvious he was not aware of his surroundings but was still among the horror from which he had escaped.

The sight of him shocked me more than the sounds that continued from his throat. Shaking myself, I stepped farther into the room. In a low steady voice, I said to him, "You are safe. Do not be afraid, nothing will harm you here." At the sound of my voice, he ceased screaming, his eyes closed, and he fell back as if in a faint. Tentatively, I approached the bed until I was standing over him. He appeared to be in a deep sleep, so I gently pulled the covers up to his chin and quietly left the room, shutting the door behind me. Sleep did not come easily after that. I told myself things were changing, and I had best prepare myself for what was to come. Strangely, the thought did not frighten me as it would have before he came. I was somewhat curious as to what tomorrow might bring.

2

Within a week, he was able, with help, to make it to the front
porch and sit for a spell in the rocking chair and enjoy the
fresh air. He had told me his name, Abram Miller, and he had been a
soldier fighting for the Confederacy. But that was all he had divulged.
Being somewhat laconic myself, I did not push him for more information. I believed in time he would come to trust me and perhaps
confide how he came to be here on this mostly deserted road.

Afraid to leave him unattended while he sat in the wooden
rocker, I would sit beside him in a chair I brought out from the
kitchen. At first, it seemed a bit awkward but gradually I grew to
enjoy the times we shared out there. There were few words spoken
between us, but I didn't mind. He seemed to notice every sound
around us, and his eyes would trail the hawks as they swooped and
dipped, hunting for prey. I brewed coffee in the mornings and strong
sugared tea for our afternoons. Gradually, we spent more and more
time sitting together on the covered porch that spanned across the
entire length of the front of the house. And, the feeling of loneliness
I had felt for so long dissipated, and I was content.

But the ghastly nightmares continued without letup. And each
night, I would hurriedly make the trek to his room to soothe him
with my voice until, exhausted, he fell again into a restless sleep.

His appetite had improved immensely, and I showed off my
cooking skills by tempting him with the recipes that had been my

father's favorites. Father's clothes were also of great use as Abram began to move about on his own. Though at first they hung loosely on his gaunt frame, he was gaining weight, and after each meal, he would thank me generously. Our days were uninterrupted; it was seldom that anyone came down the road that ran in front of my house. The road dead-ended just a short distance to the west. I was especially grateful now that visitors no longer intruded upon my privacy. I wouldn't let myself dwell on the consequences if our situation should become known to people from the community or the church. To discover a man living under my roof would surely cost me my position as a teacher and, though I cared nothing of their opinions of me personally, I was still the daughter of a preaching man, and father's reputation did matter a great deal to me.

One morning, as I followed Abram to the porch for his daily outing, I was surprised when he said, "Elizabeth, could we talk for a spell?"

"All right, if you would like to." Astonished at his willingness to have more than a casual conversation, I sat down on the caned bottom chair just a few feet from him, laid my head back, and relaxed, taking in deep breaths of the warm summer air. I was tired. Nursing him and caring for the small farm were somewhat wearing. The lack of uninterrupted sleep during the nights left me feeling drained. I kept my eyes closed and waited for him to begin, knowing it was best not to push him.

"I want you to know I appreciate all you have done for me. But I don't want to burden you any longer. You've been more than kind." He spoke slowly as if it took great effort on his part.

His words stunned me. Turning my head to face him, I stared into the deep brown eyes that had come to mean a great deal to me. I quickly tried to reassure him it was not a burdensome thing having him here.

"Well, we will see about your leaving when you are stronger and able to complete your journey. Truthfully, I don't find your company taxing. It's been some time since I've had anyone to talk to." I lowered my head, unable to keep the tears from pooling and not wanting him to see how much his presence had come to mean to me.

He did not respond and turned to look out over the vista that made up the front yard, out to the road, and beyond to the dense woods. After the silence between us grew too long, I hesitantly asked him, "Abram, if you don't mind, would you tell me where it is you plan to go? I don't even know where you come from."

He stared at me quizzically as if I had asked him a question that was beyond his comprehension and then hesitantly replied, "I guess, I don't rightly know."

"But where did you come from?" I boldly asked him, hoping to learn something of what frightened him so.

"Hell!" he stated firmly, as if that explained it all, and again turned his head away.

That was the end of our conversation. Rising, I went inside to begin our noon meal. I was afraid to ask him more questions, but my curiosity was more intense than ever. Who was this man that stirred such deep feelings in me? In the short two weeks he had been with me, I had become far too attached to this stranger.

That night, his screams awoke me as usual and this time, I didn't bother with my wrapper but ran directly to his room to quiet him. He was thrashing about on the bed, his body contorted by his struggle. I said the words that always seemed to soothe him. "Abram, you are safe. It's all right. Nothing will harm you here!" But this time, the words had no effect on him. Placing the lantern on the bedside, I leaned over him and tried to take hold of his arms. I was deeply alarmed that he was shaking as if he had the chills, and trying to warm him, I pulled the quilt up over him. Unaware of what he was doing, he kicked it off again and again.

Desperate, without thinking, I crawled onto the bed beside him and pulled him to me, hoping the warmth of my body would cause the chills to cease. At first, he resisted, but I wrapped my arms securely around him and held him firmly all the while talking in a soothing voice. Gradually, he became calmer, and relaxing, stretched his body the full length of mine. I was afraid to move, afraid to take my arms from around him as he seemed to have fallen into a deep sleep. I laid there quietly for the longest time and then, my eyes grew heavy, and I too drifted into sleep.

It was late into the night, the lantern had burned out and the room was in total darkness when I awoke to his hands caressing my body. I began to struggle against the assault, when he whispered urgently, "Please, Elizabeth, please, I need you so." I had never heard those words before, never dreamed of lying with a man, and never believed I would be loved. So, a decision was made without thought to consequences or tomorrow. I wanted this man to stay with me, wanted him to feel as I did and beyond question, wanted to ease his pain. My heart was racing with fear as I forced my body to relax and eased even closer to him and let him do whatever he wanted. There were no more words, just the motions of our bodies and the sounds that came from him, and when it was over, he rolled off me and fell into a deep dreamless sleep as I lay motionless beside him.

Tears escaped from my eyes and ran unheeded down the sides of my face, although I could not determine exactly what they were for. There had been pain, but it had not been so painful to cause me to weep. I was filled with the strangest emotions. I felt lost and bruised, not just in my body but in my spirit as well. I didn't know what I should do now or how I could possibly look upon his face in the morning. Deeply troubled, I forced myself to not think or feel anything until finally I, too, fell asleep.

When I awoke the next morning, daylight was streaming through the window. Opening my eyes, I looked to the other side of the bed expecting to see him there, but the bed was empty. My heart lurched as the thought ran through my mind, *Oh god, he is gone.* Then I heard noises coming from the kitchen and smelled bacon cooking on the stove. I hurriedly slipped to my room for my wrapper and then to the kitchen to see him bent over the skillet scrambling eggs. I stood in the doorway watching him until, as if sensing my presence, he turned from the stove, and seeing me, gave a wry awkward grin and said, "Good morning. I hope you're hungry. I thought it was about time I waited on you for a change."

Limp with relief, I fell onto the nearest chair and kept my head down, unable to look directly at him. What must he be thinking of me? For that matter, what do I think of myself? The depth of confusion surrounding me was making it hard to breathe. I was stiff and sore and knew I must look dreadful. Why hadn't I taken the time to at least brush out my hair before stumbling in here? I couldn't jump up and run out now so I remained sitting at the table with my head down like a frightened colt.

We were silent as he went about dishing up the food, pouring coffee, and finally seating himself across from me. "Do you want to talk about last night?" he said without looking directly at me.

Raising my head, I stared at the side of his face and replied, "I'm not sure there is anything to talk about. You needed me."

"Elizabeth, I know that was your first time. Did I hurt you?" His face was red with embarrassment and his voice choked with emotion.

Shaking my head no, I refrained from answering him.

"Well, let's eat our breakfast. But I want you to know you are the kindest woman I have ever met."

What I knew was he had not mentioned the word love. Somehow, I needed to hear that word from his mouth. Even though we had only been together a short period of time, I was becoming more attached to him each day, and if he did not share the same feeling for me, I thought I might shatter into tiny pieces. Did I love him? I didn't know, but we had performed an act reserved only for the marriage bed and somehow that act had changed me forever, and I didn't think I could live with the knowledge that to him it had meant very little.

That night was a repeat of the night before and the next night as well. During the day, we refrained from mentioning what occurred during the hours of the night. On the fourth night, I went back to sleeping in my old bed with the man whom I loved with every fiber of my being. There were so many emotions flying through my mind. At times I was exuberantly happy and other times panicked with fear that he would tire of me and move on. I only knew that somehow Abram had become my other half, and without him, I would never be whole again.

I was beginning to look forward to lying with Abram and tried to match his desires with my own. His nightmares continued unabated. When they dragged him back into the hell he had escaped from, my arms and my body were offered to comfort him, and after our lovemaking, he always fell into a deep dreamless sleep, and with the healing sleep, he began to truly heal, at least in body.

During our nights together, we began to talk in the darkness, as we lay side by side in the deep feather mattress bed, or rather, Abram would confide in me and I would listen intently. It became our ritual. First, the lantern would be blown out and we would become one. Then his voice, shaking with emotion, would lead me further into the hell he had somehow managed to survive. He held nothing back from me, describing in detail what was done to him.

Haunted by the terrible battles of the war itself, it was after he and the men he fought with were captured and sent to a prisoner of war camp in Chicago, Illinois, that the horror began. Camp Douglas was the Yankee's largest prisoner-of-war camp. Abram's memory was astute for the dates of every death, torture, and indecent thing they did to him and to his fellow soldiers. As he related the horrible details, I lived through each ordeal as if I had been there beside him. My tears fell silently night after night as I listened to the anguish pouring out of him. I came to believe that his pain had become mine, and his hatred against the Yankee's filled me with a fiery desire to punish them for the atrocities performed against my love.

He had no one, no family of his own since he was thirteen when his ma died. I tried to not interrupt when he related his stories as he seemed to forget I was there. But on the night he said he had no family at all, I blurted out without thinking, "Abram, what happened to your father?" There was a silence that dragged on for so long I thought he must have dozed off.

"I reckon I don't have one, at least she never spoke of anyone. I asked her once who my daddy was and she whipped me so hard I could barely sit for a week." Then he rolled over and drew his knees up to his chest and shut me out as if a door had been closed between us. I didn't interrupt him again.

Abram trusted me completely now. He oftentimes seemed eager to release the poison inside his mind, and as the gall poured out of him, I began to see a different man. He was allowing himself to laugh, and his gait was no longer slow and careful. But there were those moments when the darkness of his memories won and his soul grew heavy. Nothing I said or did could lighten his mood. When he told me of the days he spent in a room, tied at the wrists, suspended above the floor, just high enough that his feet could not reach the ground, were the worst. Hearing of those times when three guards took turns burning his body with their cigars as he hung, thrashing and screaming, were almost beyond my enduring. There did not seem to be any purpose to the questions they asked him. As if the questions were not meant to be answered but used as an excuse to torture.

And each night, as he released the hatred and shared his terrifying memories, I took them into my soul, and my hatred grew for his enemies as if I, too, had hung in that room alongside Abram. I could picture the three guards as clearly as I could my students in my classroom.

We had been together for almost a month now. I was trying to learn how not to provoke him, but fits of pique came on him at the strangest times, and during those times, he would cut me to the bone with words that were scalpel sharp. Then his mood would change and he would become contrite, begging me to forgive him, and telling me he didn't deserve someone like me, and I should just send him packing on down the road. And each time he mentioned leaving, I would begin to weep and wrap my arms around him and beg him to stay. I loved him with such intensity that it almost frightened me at times. I never voiced my love for him, believing he must be the first to declare his love, and I tried to be patient.

Each day, I felt that we were becoming closer until I came to believe that we were one—one soul, one spirit—inhabiting two bodies. When he took a deep breath, I felt the air fill my lungs and when he lay upon me, I knew nothing could separate this man from me.

I wished for a time when we were not constantly fighting a battle between the light and the darkness that would come over him. And then, it happened. All my wishes came true on one vibrant day. It was one of those rare days when everything fell into perfect harmony. The temperature did not rise above eighty-five degrees according to the thermometer on the back porch. The sky was filled with billowy white clouds, and a light breeze blew out of the north that cooled our skin.

The previous night had been a particularly good night through which Abram had slept without the customary nightmares; he was blessedly peaceful, helping me with the chores throughout the morning. As we worked side by side in the open air, he would occasionally smile broadly, lifting his face toward the sun and taking in deep breaths of the clean cool air. Suddenly, without warning, he grabbed my waist and swung me in circles until I was breathless. Laughter erupted from him as we spun around on the barren dirt of the garden plot, and my laughter mixed with his. We held each other tightly and stood swaying until the dizziness ceased. But his arms continued to hold me close to him and then he lowered his head and kissed me for the longest time. At that moment, I knew what Father meant when he spoke of the joy of heaven.

I was disappointed when that very night, the nightmares returned. I was coming to believe that it was imperative for him to relate all of the horrible atrocities he had endured and only then would he be able to heal. His mind was like a wound that had become infected with gangrene, and by clearing it out, we might be able to live our lives with happiness.

Abram's enemies had become my enemies; his torturers were now my torturers. When he uttered the name of Abraham Lincoln through clenched teeth, I would be overcome with anger at the man who started the horrible war that had destroyed most of the south. Until Abram came into my life, I gave no thought to a war that had little effect on us here in Indian Territory.

Over time, I was gradually extracting the details of Abram's prison life. He and those of his company, who had survived their last battle, were taken prisoner and arrived at Camp Douglas on January 26, 1863. On that day, fifteen hundred confederate prisoners arrived. The next day, thirteen hundred more came, and on January 30, another fifteen hundred weary and wounded soldiers were brought in.

The magnitude of men held captive in that far off northern camp so overwhelmed me I felt faint when he related the numbers.

At first, I was skeptical when he would recite so many figures, but Abram was surprisingly gifted with numbers. He had little formal schooling but numbers remained in his mind, and years later, he could recall them with clarity. During February, 387 died as temperatures dropped to minus twenty degrees. Small pox and other diseases were widespread and by March, twenty-nine prisoners and nineteen guards had died of small pox alone. By April, the death toll of prisoners reached 1,084. If it was not the raging diseases, then the brutal guards killed without mercy.

A fiend, named Captain Webb Sponable, was responsible for many of the most horrific deaths. He ordered the guards to torture under the excuse of retrieving secret plans of the Confederacy. Abram was one of many that Captain Sponable had thrown into the "White Oak Dungeon", an underground room, eighteen feet square, lit by one small barred window near the very top. The only entry or exit was through a hatch in the ceiling. The room was packed with so many bodies it was impossible to lay down, and without a proper toilet, the intolerable stench from the bowels of the soldiers was almost unbearable. Gruel was lowered by a rope once a day, and only the ones positioned nearest the hatch came away with food to survive another day.

The lucky ones, those who died in the prisoner-of-war camp, were given over into the hands of an unscrupulous undertaker who sold many of their bodies to medical schools. The rest were buried in shallow graves without coffins, or dumped into Lake Michigan until their bodies began to wash up on shore, and the citizens of the metropolis complained. When approached with that news, printed on the front page of the local newspaper, the undertaker swore under oath that all bodies had been sent back to their families.

It was the times when his fellow soldiers suffered along with him that kept him alive. They could endure almost anything as long as they were together. But the times when he was alone with the guards and tortured for hours on end killed his spirit, and he begged for death. Many times, he was carried to the makeshift hospital where he was treated so viciously by the doctors he grew to fear them almost as much as he feared the guards.

There was a glimmer of lightness beginning in him as he released the ghastly memories, and darkness grew in me as I took them from him. In the days and weeks that followed, I kept my anguish over what they had done to him to myself. But in the darkness of the nights when his nightmares brought us both to the edge of insanity, my hatred rose with each atrocity.

Abram's dark moods during the day were becoming less and less frequent, and the joy of being together was precious to us both. There were picnics under the dogwood tree and fishing in the pond followed by the delicious meals of fried bass and potatoes. Our almost nightly lovemaking was something I looked forward to now that I had grown used to it. But the word I wanted to hear so badly never left Abram's lips.

One night, after a particularly rough nightmare, I held him close to me and surprised myself as I whispered the words, "I love you, Abram. I wish I could take these visions from you, my darling."

His body tensed, and I was afraid he was angry with me, but he took a deep breath and replied shakily, "I know you do, Elizabeth, and I know you to be the kindest creature there is." But the words "I love you" were not spoken.

The summer was drawing to a close. Soon it would be time for me to return to teaching at the school house in town. Over the summer, I made several trips into town for supplies, but Abram never accompanied me. We both knew it best if no one was aware he was living with me at the little farm. And he seemed to be content with only my company. He never complained of not having other men folk to talk to, and I was loathed to share him with anyone else.

I did try a few times to speak of the future and what it might mean to the two of us, but Abram would quickly change the subject, and I was content believing our future was secure as long as we were together.

One evening, I had supper ready and went to the parlor to call him to the table. Stopping short in the parlor door, I was surprised to see him sitting at father's rolltop desk with Father's bible laid out in front of him. He was shaking his head as he flipped through the pages before him. Walking over to him, I stood looking down as he continued to turn the pages randomly. He was so engrossed in the book I startled him as I laid my hand on his shoulder. Jerking his head up, he guiltily said, "I'm sorry, Elizabeth. I was only looking at it. I wasn't gonna harm it any."

"Oh, it's fine, Abram. I didn't know you liked to read the Bible."

"Can't say that I do really. Truth is, I never got hold of one before."

"Well, you're welcome to Father's. I'm sure he wouldn't mind."

"No, no I can't really understand most of the words so don't guess it would do me much good."

"Abram, do you believe in God?" I asked him.

Taking a deep breath, he hesitated, contemplating the question, and then looking up at me with the gravest expression on his face, he said, "Yes, I reckon there is. So many of the men I saw die would call out to God to save them and then some would get this strange smile on their face and just let go and die. Where I've been was a hell for sure, so there must be the opposite, like God and heaven. It's like the sun and the moon. Like love and hate, like laughing and crying. Isn't that right, Elizabeth?"

I was so astounded by his answer, I was speechless. Finally, I said, "You may be right, Abram. Now come in to supper."

Seated at the table across from me, he had one more thing to say on the subject. "One thing I know for sure is, there are angels! And I'm sitting right across from one right now."

3

It was almost time to start the dreary chore of teaching again. I had never before dreaded school starting, but now I loathed anything that took me away from Abram for a single moment. I used to look forward to seeing my students at the beginning of each new year. I suppose I lived somewhat vicariously through them. Now I had no reason to envy anyone, but I deeply resented even the thought of time away from Abram. We had shared our lives for almost three months and each day, I needed him more and more and loved him more and more.

He had been particularly jovial the past few days. The darkness seemed to have retreated from us both. He had actually slept through the night for several nights in a row and spoke of planting a fall crop to help us through the winter. The half wild horse was tame as a kitten with him, and Abram took to riding her across the pasture as fast as she could run. I would stand in the barn door and watch them as his hair streamed back from his face, and a smile locked on his features as the rebel yell came from his throat and rebounded around us. When they were finished, he would come to me, leading the mare, who obediently followed behind him shaking her mane with happiness.

It was almost September, and I began to gather up supplies I would need for teaching. Each year, I saved them for the next year and occasionally, new tools were added as the superintendent of the district deemed appropriate. I taught eight grades in the one room school house. There were seldom over twenty students in a given year, but the town was growing. Over the summer, I noticed at least three new families shopping at the stores. It didn't matter how many I must teach, the only thing that mattered to me was the time I spent with Abram.

I dreaded that first Monday and leaving Abram alone at the farm. He had not been far from my side our whole time together. Sleep had not come easily that Sunday night, and I arose before the sun was completely up, made us coffee, and stood on the front porch and watched the colors of the sky change from gray to hues of oranges and golds. Breakfast had no taste, and I couldn't force myself to eat. Abram noticed my reticence and asked me cautiously, "Are you feeling all right, Elizabeth?"

I nodded my head but did not trust my voice; I was close to the edge of having myself a good cry. Reading my thoughts, he came around the table and pulled me to him. "I'll be waiting right here when you get home." Looking up at the face that meant so much to me, I returned the smile that played on his lips. Letting me go, he said, "You go finish getting ready and I'll clean up."

Feeling better, I hurried to the bedroom and dressed quickly. He was waiting for me on the porch and stepping out, I clung to him until he laughingly pushed me from him. Turning me around, he gave me a sharp smack across my bottom and said, "Away with you, woman. I have work that needs to be done and so do you." Laughing with him, I hurried out the gate and down the dirt road toward town.

The long walk into town seemed to fly by. I knew the quicker I got to the school, the quicker the time would pass. But it seemed an unendurably long day. The hours crept by as if the old clock hanging on the back wall stopped every few minutes. Finally, I could release the children who were as anxious to leave as I was. Tidying up, as I must do at the end of each day, I quickly got through the last of the chores and hurriedly left for the two-and-a-half-mile walk home.

It was exceptionally warm, almost the warmest day of the summer, but I rushed just the same. By the time the house came into sight, I was sweating profusely and out of breath. As I hurried forward, I saw Abram leap from his place on the porch and, bounding down the steps, throw open the gate and sprint toward me. We met in the middle of the road, almost in the exact spot I had found him three months ago. I dropped the parcels I had been carrying, and holding out my arms, he rushed into them and held me so tight I could barely breathe. Without releasing me from his arms, he lowered his head, and as his lips found mine, I was happier than I had ever been. The kiss lasted for the longest time, and I felt we were bonded together as never before. Finally, we released each other, and he stooped over and retrieved my packages.

Looking up at me, he said, "I didn't know how lonesome I was gonna be without you. I'm glad you're home."

Smiling down at him, I said, "I missed you, too."

With our arms around each other, we walked to the house and for the first time, in daylight, he led me to the bedroom. Laying me on top of the spread, he made love to me with the sun streaming through the window. The old chintz curtain was billowing in as the breeze cooled our heated bodies. We laid there for a time without speaking, and I was filled with love and happiness.

The next few days were more of the same. Each day, our time together was lovelier, and I was elated. He lavished attention on me and often surprised me with little things that made me smile—the wild flowers that adorned the table when I got home from school, the brown betty he had made from the dried apples in the root cellar, and the sweet words he whispered in my ear as I drifted off to sleep each night. I was content. I was the luckiest of all women even without the words of undying love. I reasoned some men just found it hard to express themselves, but Abram showed me in so many ways each day that he loved me.

It rained hard during Thursday night. The roads were muddy and filled with little pools of water. For the first time, Abram insisted I ride the mare to school so as not to get myself muddied and so I would get home faster that afternoon. He saddled her up and led her around to the front gate, then waited for me on the porch, as he had each morning. I hurried as I swung the screen door open and joined him. Giving him a quick hug, I expected to be released and escorted to the waiting mare. But his arms held me and drew me closer to him until I felt every part of his body.

I wasn't sure what had brought this on and looked up at him. He had the strangest expression on his face, but seeing my dismay, he brought his face down to mine and kissed me deeply. Laughing, I drew back and said, "Abram, I'm going to be late. You'll just have to wait for more when I get home." He laughed along with me and with his arm firmly around my waist, he walked me to the mare, helped me mount, and handed me the reins.

As I reached for them, he took hold of my hand and looking up at me with the soberest expression said, "Elizabeth, you know that I love you?"

Shocked and speechless, I nodded my head up and down. He smiled and stepping back waved me off.

I was stunned by his words and for a while was dizzy with happiness. But by the time I reached the school, I had become somewhat uneasy. As the day slowly passed, I went over and over the moment he had uttered the words I had waited so long to hear.

My mind was not on the curriculum, so I gave each grade reading assignments to do as I began to feel an intense apprehension growing inside me. The feeling that something was terribly wrong grew as the day slugged by. I should have been happy, gleeful, but a growing fear was setting in my heart. I argued with myself, telling myself I was being foolish and should be ashamed for letting my imagination get the best of me.

But as the hours dragged by, my throat became too dry to swallow, and I felt like I was choking. Drinking a cup of water from the wooden bucket did nothing to quench my thirst, and my hands were trembling so hard that water sloshed over the tin cup as I brought it to my lips. By two o'clock, I could no longer ignore the growing sense that something dreadful was going to happen.

I closed school early and sent the stunned students home. Without completing my usual chores, I climbed onto the mare and set out for home in a dead run. The pools of water from last night's rain had dried up, but the road remained muddy, making it difficult for the running mare. I urged her faster and faster causing her to be running at full speed. She was heaving mightily when we got to the house.

Abram was not in his usual place on the porch. Leaping off the exhausted horse, I was hollering his name before I got the front door opened. I ran from one room to the next screaming for him, but only silence answered me throughout the house. His clothing and all of his belongings I had given him were still in their place. Nothing was out of order, but my skin was crawling, and a horrible dread was threatening to cause me to faint.

Trying to calm myself, I walked out the back door and shading my eyes scanned the pasture and the small garden plot. The garden hoe was leaning against the post rail like it was waiting for Abram to reclaim it and finish hoeing the weeds. It was eerily quiet, even the birds were silent.

The horse came slowly around the house, head down, trailing the reins from her halter with white lather standing out along her neck and withers like crystals of salt. I picked up the reins and led the exhausted mare to the horse trough for a badly needed drink. The water was very low in the trough.

Abram must not have filled it this morning.

I turned around in a slow circle, my eyes desperate to see him walking toward me, but there was no sign of him. A feeling of despair was growing inside me like a dark cancer. My throat was so dry I could barely swallow, and I had begun to shake as if I had a chill.

I waited for the mare to finish drinking, and when she raised her head, I loosened the saddle and dragged it off her and led her to the pasture gate. Removing the halter, I turned her loose into the pasture; the grass was still damp from last night's rain. Turning around, I walked back to the saddle lying on the ground. Picking it up, I headed toward the barn.

I heard a strange noise as I approached the barn door, a weird creaking sound, which raised the hair along the back of my neck.

Dropping the saddle to the ground, I slowly stepped over the low threshold and cautiously entered the darkness that enveloped the old building. At first, I could see nothing, but as my eyes grew accustomed to the dimness, an outline drew my eyes upward. I knew—knew without doubt—what was making the dreadful sound.

His back was to me as he hung from the rafter and his body gently swayed from the breeze that blew through the door. It was his body on the end of the rope, draped over the rafter that was causing the rope to grind on the wood creating the horrid sound.

I no longer had control over my body. I sank to the hay-covered floor and knelt there as if praying to the God my father had loved so dearly. The world stopped turning, and time ceased there in the old barn that held the body of the man who was my life.

At first, I was numb, but then I began to shake violently. As the chills abated, I felt heat engulf me until I was covered in sweat. I told my legs to raise me up, but they were limp. I opened my mouth to scream and scream, but no sounds came out. Even my eyes would not obey me. Though I begged them to close, they were glued on Abram's body as it swayed gently in the dim barn. The grating sound grew louder and louder.

I'm not sure how long I remained kneeling on the hard floor, but gradually, I made it to my feet and walked around to the front of his body. His face was blue, not the handsome sun-tanned face I had grown used to. I forced myself to look at the lifeless eyes, opened wide as if he could see me below him. The expression on his bloated face must have been similar to how he looked when he was being tortured.

I was absurdly calm as I examined every inch of his face and then his hands. The hands that had touched my body, caressed me lovingly, and helped me onto the mare, only this morning. These same hands that had tossed the rope over the rafter and dragged the sawhorse underneath. I looked behind him and stared at the broken sawhorse lying on its side where it landed when his feet kicked the support out from under himself.

Stepping back, I asked him, "Were you sorry when you kicked over the sawhorse? Did you think of me finding you here? I'm really getting angry at you, Abram!" My voice sounded strained in my own ears.

Turning around, I picked up the small axe hanging on one of the stalls and climbing the ladder to the top of the loft, stepped out onto the rafter that rose high above the barn floor. Balancing carefully, I walked cautiously out to where the rope was tied around the beam. I hacked at it once but nothing happened. I hit it again with all my strength. This time, the rope was cut through, and with a loud thud, Abram's body fell to the floor. I remained where I was and listened to the normal sounds of an ordinary day without the maddening squeak of the rope rubbing against the rafter.

Balancing myself, I backed slowly to the solid planks of the loft, returned down the ladder, and carefully hung the axe back where it belonged.

Oblivious to time, I squatted down a few feet from his body and peered at the still form sprawled awkwardly on the barn floor. Patiently, I waited for him to sit up and explain why he had left me. I was determined to wait until I got an answer. I don't know how long I waited, but it must have been hours later when he began to speak, not in his usual voice, but from deep inside of me, as if he had entered my body.

He patiently explained that the depravity he and his brothers-in-arms had endured as prisoners was so severe the weakest of them could not live, and it was not fair that he did not die and go along with them.

"But, Abram, you love me and I love you, which changes everything. You need to come back now!" I knew if I explained it all to him, he would get up and we would pretend this had never happened.

He continued as if I had not spoken. "Elizabeth, I realize now that I died there in that prison along with the others, but God must have wanted me to know, at least once in my life, what it was like to be loved. And He sent me here to find you. Remember that I love you."

The voice faded and then was gone. Throughout the long night, alone in the pitch darkness, with nothing but his words running through my mind, they resonated over and over. I sat there studying on each word until the sun rose above the horizon and the barn was filled with an eerie dim light. Dust motes swirled around on the slight breeze.

When I had mulled it over and determined a plan, I rose painfully from my position, and after relieving myself in the outhouse, went to our bedroom and retrieved the quilt I used to drag Abram from the road to the house on the day I found him.

Taking it back to the barn, I wrapped it around him and began to drag him toward the flowering dogwood tree on the knoll. He was much heavier than when I first found him in the road, and I repeatedly had to stop and rest. The sun was past the noon hour by the time I had dragged him where I wanted him.

Strangely, I wasn't hungry, but thirst became a problem. On the way back to the barn to get a shovel, I drew water from the well and drank my fill of the cool liquid. Taking the shovel up to the knoll, I began the arduous task of digging a grave for my love.

Mother told me the story of the dogwood tree when she planted the bare little root stock that looked like nothing more than a dead twig. "It was the great dogwood tree that was cut for timber to make the cross they hung our Savior on. And from that day to this, the dogwood tree has never grown large enough to be used for such a horrible purpose again." She smiled down at me as she related the tale. "And that is why the flowers of this little tree will look like the shape of the cross when it blooms." She was right. The blossoms that filled the tree were white, and the four petals were shaped like a cross. There were no blossoms now; they had matured into green leaves, which were already beginning to turn to autumn colors.

I dug for hours and hours before the grave was deep enough and wide enough to hold him comfortably. I did want him to be comfortable even though I was still upset with him for what he had done. Sitting down beside him, I rested for a spell. Then I walked slowly to the well and drank my fill again before climbing back to the knoll to finish laying Abram to rest. I almost fell into the grave with him as I rolled him into the coolness of the dark earth.

There is a particularly pungent smell that comes from the depths of the earth. It's not unpleasant but distinctly earthy. I wonder if the smell gets stronger the deeper you go? Hmm, I will ponder on that when I have time.

Finally, satisfied with his position, I began to fill the grave with the soil that would cover and protect him from prying eyes and any varmints that nosed around. It took me almost as long to cover him over as it did to dig the grave in the first place. Fatigue had overtaken me by the time I had pounded the loose earth down firmly, so no one would ever know he lay beneath their feet. Then, forcing myself to keep moving, I dragged stones, weeds, and planted some undergrowth over the newly mounded grave, hiding it completely.

Wearily, I leaned against the shovel handle and noticed that it was now dusk. The sun was almost set and the moon had risen above the tree line. The animals were fretting for their food, and no matter how exhausted I was, they needed to eat. Even the mare was snorting for more water in her trough. Without rational thought, I went through the motions and completed my duties.

4

Dragging myself into the house, I crawled onto our bed. I fell into a deep sleep and did not awaken until early Sunday morning. The moment I awoke, a plan had totally formed in my mind and I knew exactly what must be done. Unfortunately, it would have to wait until tomorrow as the Sabbath would never do.

This is a beautiful morning. The air is crisp, cool, and clean like an Easter morning. Fixing a large breakfast, I sat at the kitchen table and gorged myself until I could hardly rise and clean up the mess I had made. Then in a whirlwind of activity, I scrubbed the entire house, even taking the time to wash the linens on our bed.

Everywhere I looked, it sparkled and shone, and at last, I was satisfied with the effort. The day was mostly gone as the hours of cleaning had eaten it away.

Carrying the wash tub into the kitchen, I drew water from the well and after several trips had enough to satisfy myself. I heated the water on the stove, until it started to simmer, and then carefully filled the tub to almost overflowing with the steaming water. Stripping off the old house dress I gingerly tested the water, first with a foot and when that was bearable climbed slowly into the tub. Sinking down into it, I let it cover my entire body. I languished, there in the hot water, until my skin began to wrinkle, and the water was too cool to be comfortable. Quickly, I washed the grime and sweat from my body and scrubbed my hair until it was squeaky clean. Stepping briskly from the tub, I dried myself off and dusted the sweet smelling talc over my skin until the scent filled the room.

Not bothering to dress, I carried buckets of the dirty water and threw them out the back door until I could drag the wash tub to the door. I tipped it over and let it run down the stoop out into the yard. I put everything back in its place and finished by drying the kitchen floor with the towel I had used to dry my body. Still naked, I carried the wet towel outside to the clothesline and hung it firmly with the wooden pins. Laughing at my boldness, I marched back into the house.

It was getting late, the sun was setting, and the sunset was especially lovely this evening. I brewed fresh coffee and taking a cup out with me, sat in mother's rocker, with my wrapper hugged tightly around me, and let myself relax, content with what I had accomplished and confident in what was left to be done.

Before retiring for the night, I laid out my best dress and my Sunday shoes, saved for years to be worn only at Sunday services. Everything good was always saved for very special occasions which was befitting, considering…

Knowing I had done everything that needed to be done, I went to the small bedroom and not bothering to turn the coverlet down, laid across the bed, falling asleep immediately.

I awoke early before the sun rose. Lighting the coal oil lamp on the nightstand, I carried it with me to light the way and walked slowly through the rooms as if seeing them for the first time. Everything around me seemed different than it had the day before. The furniture in the rooms I had lived in all of my life looked strangely out of place as if we no longer knew each other. There was no sense of belonging in this house, no feeling of familiarity with the objects that Mother and Father had accumulated during their years together.

It did not alarm me. Walking from room to room, I ran my hands over the items that should have had some meaning to me. But instead, they seemed to weigh me down, as if reaching out to hang onto me. It was a stifling, disquieting feeling, and I hurriedly went into the bedroom I had shared with Abram. The sun had risen, filling the room with light, so I blew out the lantern. I stared at the bed where I had learned what it was to be loved by a man. A smile played across my lips, and a hint of laughter escaped as I ran my fingers over the bed coverlet. Here in this room is where I felt the closest to Abram. I could feel his presence and knew he was anxious for me to finish my task.

I quickly dressed in my best clothes and brushing my hair until it shone, I wound a length of ribbon under the long tresses in the back and up each side and tied the ends to form a bow on the top of my head. I heard Abram laughing at my attempt to make myself beautiful and looking in the cloudy mirror saw the reflection of a glowing, somewhat attractive, woman staring back at me.

As I stepped out the back door, I noticed the sun had risen above the horizon. I headed for the horse trough to fill it with water for the mare and then fed the chickens wandering around the yard. I had neglected eating breakfast but was not hungry, only anxious to finish the chores and get to my plan. Stopping for a moment, I tilted my head back and closing my eyes, I felt the coolness of the breeze as it caressed my skin. I had never felt so alive.

Then turning toward the barn, I took long strides toward the door. Each step and movement had been carefully planned, and I immediately saw what I needed.

A long length of hemp rope was coiled around a hook on the wall by the stalls. Pulling it down, I sat on a bale of hay and expertly made a loop in the shape of a noose on one end. Then looking up at the rafter that Abram had used to start his journey, I climbed the ladder once more.

Standing on the solid floor of the loft, I gently pulled the noose over my head and tightened it so it would not slip. Then taking a deep breath, I gingerly stepped onto the rafter, and carefully balancing, walked slowly to the middle of the long beam. Knowing this was the trickiest part of my plan, I moved cautiously as I lowered myself down to tie the other end of the rope securely to the rafter. It was surprisingly easy as if everything in the universe was helping me on my way to Abram.

Straightening up, I stood tall, and staring straight ahead, I told Abram, "I understand now, my love. Abraham Lincoln began this horrible war, and his terrible men murdered you before you came to me, and they are guilty of murdering me as well. But they cannot ever separate us again." Seething with rage over what they had done to us, I stepped out toward Abram's waiting arms…

I am so weary of reliving this over and over. Each time, my memories take me from the beginning of my life to that unthinkable day when he chose to leave me alone and racked with grief, nothing changes. It is the same each time. Why am I here? That moment, when I stepped out to what I believed was his waiting arms, and then… there was nothing, only darkness until I awoke and found myself here. Abram was not waiting for me. I only remember being here in this place without knowing how I got here or why I am a prisoner confined here as he was a prisoner so long ago.

She did not see the tall figure looming over her or hear the sound of its massive wings as they spread out from its back. A look of deep concern came across his ageless face as he rose above the figure he had watched over from the time she was an infant. Barael soared high into the heavens to report the latest news on his charge.

Standing before the great archangel Michael, Barael sadly related the same identical message he had delivered countless times.

"Do not be so dejected, Barael, you know He has a plan to release her from her bondage. Soon, very soon, her time will be over, and He will reveal all to her, and then you will witness her deep joy and happiness." Michael tried to console this loyal soldier.

"Thank you, Michael. It cannot come soon enough. I pray my next charge will have great faith. Without their faith in the Father and the Son, we are without our full strength to protect them from the demonic legions. It is disheartening to be unable to fight and deliver our charges out of the hands of the evil one."

"I know, this has been a most difficult time for you as well as your charge."

Barael's head jerked up and with a troubled expression etched on his face, declared, "I care deeply for this particular human He assigned to me, but I'm afraid I have been of little use to her. And the demons continue to torment her constantly—demons of regret, anger, hatred, sorrow, and worst of all, the vicious demon that sucks the faith from her! Their stench overpowers me at times. Their rancid, putrid odor used to alert me, they were somewhere around. Now I almost live with them!"

These last words were uttered with an angst that saddened Michael. The stoop of Barael's shoulders testified to the weight of his dilemma. His great body remained strong, and as a tested warrior, his abilities were without question. But her lack of faith had left him without his full angelic powers. He was severely hampered in his ability to shield her from the demonic forces around her. And watching her suffering was taking a deep toll on the loyal protector.

"Barael, the time is coming. The others will soon join you, and the task for you, warrior angels, is of great importance to the Master. There will be a time when you will be set free of these shackles, and when that time comes, a legion of warriors will be at your side to rid the demons from them all. For now, you must refrain from showing yourself as too powerful. Only make sure the demons surrounding her do not go too far! In the meantime, you must wait. I know you will remain faithful. Take heart, my friend."

Nodding his head in acknowledgment, Barael stood tall, no longer beaten down, but reassured by Michael's words. "I will return to her now," he said as his great wings spread out from his back. He dove down through the heavens and the firmaments to the sky above the earth and down to the small cemetery where his charge continued to be tormented daily by demons that had lost their fear of the once mighty warrior.

Michael stood silently watching as Barael descended back to earth. A hint of a smile played across his features as he thought of what was to come. Barael and the legions of angels God has assigned to His children will be greatly surprised and they, along with all the Host of Heaven, will soon be celebrating at the throne.

But not yet… not quite yet.

PART 2

1916

"Jeffrey MacCreary, Jeffrey MacCreary! Get your head off your desk right this minute!" I heard her voice coming from a far off distant place. Raising my head, I stared groggily at Miss Taylor. The color of her face attested to how mad I had made her by drifting off to sleep in the middle of the history hour. She was tall and stood ramrod straight like someone had nailed a two by four to her back. She loomed over me, her mouth set in a tight grim line. I had never seen her smile, and I figured by the set of her jaw, today was not going to be an exception.

"All right, young man. This time I will have to punish you!" She whirled around, and striding back to her desk at the front of the classroom, picked up a twelve-inch ruler and marched back to stand at my side. "Hold out your hands!" Her voice was raised a notch, shriller than her usual deep manly voice, and by the stance of her legs, she was getting ready to shed some blood today—my blood!

Looking around at the deathly silent classroom, I didn't see one ally who would be brave enough to try to talk her out of whoppin' me. She stood over me, poised with the ruler raised, and I had no time to think things over. It was either get my knuckles rapped or maybe even be forced to lean over my desk and give her a larger target, or get out. I chose the latter.

Jumping up from my seat, I grabbed her by both her arms, and turning her around, plunked her down in my chair. She was so shocked her mouth gaped wide open and the bun on top of her head came loose and her thin grey hair fell down over her face. She looked like she had been stung by a beehive full of bees. She sputtered like a car running out of gas, and the class busted out with laughter. I just kind of froze and stared at her sitting there like she was one of us kids. She finally found her voice and let it out! Miss Taylor was screaming at the top of her lungs when I lit out the door. I could still hear her a full block away, and I was running at full speed.

I was halfway home before I slowed down to a walk. I didn't know how fast ole' Miss Taylor could run. I'd never seen her do more than a fast march, but I wouldn't put it past her to be a sprinter. Figuring she must have decided to catch me in the morning, I moseyed down to a slow crawl. Walking the last mile and a half home gave me time to think. If Ma and Pa found out about this, I was in for a heap of trouble. Maybe Miss Taylor would be satisfied with a whipping tomorrow. The thought of how mad she would be by morning and being made an example in front of the class made my stomach curl up in knots.

Truth be told, I didn't need any more schoolin'. I'd already spent more time in school than Pa thought was necessary. It was Ma who insisted I get an education and when she wanted something, Pa never had the heart to deny her. They were two of the most different people, but they seemed to put up with each other's point of view without taking it too personal.

Her people were educated, and they expected their only daughter to acquire a proper education and become an accomplished wife to an equally well-educated, intelligent man, preferably somewhat well-off. Her three brothers were obedient young men and made the entire family breathe a sigh of relief when they graduated from esteemed colleges and became successful businessmen. They married proper wives and had the correct number of perfect children. The brothers were more than half-grown when Ma was born.

Ma was the youngest and had come along as a complete surprise to her stiff-necked parents who were somewhat embarrassed by the whole episode of her birth. But once she came onto the scene, she was expected to uphold the family values and live up to their standards. She was a proper and obedient young lady, until a young handsome lad drove his team up the street to their front door and delivered his farm raised produce at the back door. He had been there several times previously, but this time, she happened to be in the kitchen talking to the cook.

Opening the door, she stood face to face with the grinning farmer who, upon seeing her, quickly set down his box of groceries and pulling off his wide brimmed hat, made a low sweeping, exaggerated bow.

The whole performance caused her to break out with laughter. Pa, never one to be bashful, joined right in with her, and the two of them stood on the small stoop so close they were almost in each other's arms. She told me, "I had never laughed so freely before, and my heart was given to your Pa right that minute." They were bonded for life on that very day. At least that was the story she told me over and over when I'd beg her to tell me how she met Pa, how she had disobeyed her entire family because she loved Pa more than anything in the whole wide world, except for me, of course.

Pa had pretty much the same story to tell, but his stories were always shorter. Ma could spend all of an hour describing her thoughts on most anything and everything.

According to Ma, Pa was kind of a success himself. He was only twenty-two years old when he first set eyes on Ma. He already owned his own land, and it had a two-story white clapboard house sitting close to the road with a white fence all the way around it. Pa, like me, was an only child, and he got it when his folks passed on. It had a mortgage, but he was current with his payments, and the livestock was free and clear.

Our farm is only twenty-five miles from where Ma was raised; it might as well have been a thousand. Her home was in a large city that was the county seat and the state capital; even the county was a different one than where we lived. We lived in Lincoln County, named after the esteemed president, and her folks lived in Oklahoma City in Oklahoma County.

I have always believed that people who dwelled there were a little dull minded since they couldn't think of anything more interesting to name the city that was the state capital. But it had its very own newspaper, which didn't impress Pa, since he couldn't read or write worth a whit. He said, "You can't learn how to plow a row, or deliver a calf, or plant a garden, sittin' inside a school house." But he never let Ma hear him telling me that.

Every time he got a wagon full of produce, he'd drive the team to her town and camp down along the river where he stayed until his entire load was sold off. And each time, he stood waiting anxiously on her back stoop; he was afraid she wouldn't be home or wouldn't have time to say a few words to him. Then there was that special day when as Ma said, "The stars aligned in the heavens, the sun was just right, not too hot, a soft breeze was blowing and big white clouds billowed overhead," and your Pa said, "How would you like to go fishing down at the river?" And she, bold as brass, replied, "I surely would!" And they spent the whole afternoon sitting and talking and falling in love right there on the river bank until it was near dusk and they headed back.

She was in for a whale of misery once she got home. When they came into view, her father was pacing back and forth on the front porch, chewing a big ole cigar. Seeing her coming down the street, sitting up so proud on the wagon seat beside Pa, was more than he could stand. He ran down the front steps and yelled at Pa until the entire neighborhood heard him, "How dare you spend the day with my daughter without a chaperone! You stay away from her and away from my home. If I ever catch you around here again, I'll have the law on you!" He raised his fist as if to give Pa a what for, but thought better of it when Pa's hands turned into fist and he didn't back up an inch.

Ma was down off the seat before Pa could give her aide, and she walked right up to her furious father, and planting her feet firmly apart, took up for Pa, saying, "Father, stop it! It wasn't Sean's fault. I asked him to take me fishing, and he was nice enough to take me."

Her argument only added fuel to an already blazing fire, and for a moment, he raised his hand to strike his daughter. Then seeing the look on Pa's face, he settled for screaming at her to go inside the house. She remained where she was until Pa told her, "Go on, Emily.

Mind your Pa." Crying hard, she raced into the house. The two men faced each other with hatred between them until Pa turned away and climbed up on the wagon seat. Turning the team around, he kept them at a slow walk as they moved away from the angry man still standing in the middle of the street. Neighbors stood on porches and in front yards watching the spectacle until the team was out of sight.

When he headed down the brick paved street, Pa could hear Ma's screams until he got out of sight. I guess they both went plumb crazy during that night, thinking they would not be able to see each other again. But Ma had set her mind on having the young farmer, and before daylight, she had packed her things in a woolen tote, quietly let herself out of the house, and walked all the way to the river to find him.

He tried to reason her out of her decision, but once she made up her mind, there was no stopping her. They pulled out as fast as they could get his gear packed and loaded, and by noon, they were miles from her hometown. They camped out that night in a little glen alongside the road. Pa knew he wanted to spend the rest of his life with this young woman by his side. She was only fifteen, but she was hell-bent on staying with him, so before they went to sleep, he had asked her to marry him. Ma knew that was what she had wanted from the time she opened the back door, and he had tipped his hat to her.

The next morning, they set off again before daybreak, and keeping a steady pace made it to the small town where we live now. The local justice of the peace married them without a single question.

She never said, but I guessed, when they found her missing, her father wrote her out of the family history book, and for all intents and purposes, she never existed to him. I don't think Ma missed him much, but when she talked about her mother, she would tear up and I'd try to get her to think about something else.

When she ran off and married Pa, they shut the family door on her and wouldn't let her back in no matter how hard she tried. She thought for sure they would open it a crack when I came along. But no, they wanted no more to do with her, and, for sure, not us. I could tell it broke her heart to not be able to see or talk to her mother again, especially when I was born. She had saved all my baby clothes in an old cedar chest that had belonged to my grandmother. I knew she kept them because she hoped that someday her Ma might come to visit. But that never happened.

For some strange reason, I was the only kid they had, and I didn't come along until they had been married several years, long enough for them to give up on ever having any youngun's. But it can be real hard when you're the only kid and all their hopes are piled on your shoulders. The problem was they didn't have the same hopes, so I was always disappointing one or the other of them. Ma wanted me to be a standout in my studies, but I must have taken after Pa. I didn't care much for school and would have quit a long time ago except for her.

Slowing my steps as I got closer to home, I was deep in thought, thinking about how tough it was trying to please them. The more I thought on it, the more I came to realize that I was pretty much out of luck even trying to please them. The real truth is, I can't please both of them, and it's not my fault. They can't make up their minds what they want out of me. So, gritting my teeth, I made up my mind, right then, to just do what I wanted for a change. After all, I'm almost sixteen, that's grown up for sure. I am somewhat thin, but I'm tall for my age, and I'm a scrapper as anyone will tell you.

Making up my mind made me feel a little better about what I had done to Miss Taylor, but how I was going to tell Ma and Pa what I'd done was another matter. I decided to do what I usually did and let them hear about it from someone else. That settled things to my satisfaction, but I had a little trouble quieting that voice inside me that was trying to tell me to fess up as soon as I got in the door. I slowed down a bit more so I wouldn't get home earlier than usual from school.

I smelled the yeast bread before I started up the steps onto the porch. Ma had baked bread, and it was cooling on the kitchen table. I quit thinking about the afternoon's events and felt the hunger pangs stirring in my stomach. I was near starving as soon as I laid eyes on those brown loaves. "Ma, can I have a couple of slices with some butter?"

"Jeffrey, don't you ever get filled up?" She was smiling and already had the bread knife in her hand. She's probably the prettiest mother anywhere around. Sometimes, just looking at her made me feel good. And those two thick slabs of fresh bread, slathered in soft butter, made me feel even better. I was trying real hard not to think about tomorrow when the news of what I'd done would catch up to me.

It didn't take near as long as I thought, less than a day, which was pretty quick even for our gossipy town. I thought for sure no one would be telling on me this soon, but we had just finished our supper when we heard a car coming down the road. Miss Taylor and two school board members drove up close to the house in a fine 1915 Empire touring car. It belonged to our banker and head of the school board, George Vernon Whitman, and as everybody in town knew, he would stop you on the street and espouse the merits of his automobile to anyone who would listen.

The three of us walked out onto the porch as the remarkable car came to a halt a few feet from the steps. It was a joy to behold! I ignored the three individuals getting out of the Empire. I didn't look in Ma or Pa's direction. My full attention was centered on the automobile. Ducking my head, I went around to the other side of the car and looked it over close, running my hands over the sleek hood and sticking my head into the interior to sniff the leather that smelled like a fine saddle. I had never been this close to it before. I was so busy admiring the auto that I almost forgot about the three adults who were marching up the porch steps to talk to Ma and Pa.

Miss Charlotte Taylor was old, at least close to forty. She was a teacher because she was a spinster and that's what spinsters do. It was no surprise to me that she had remained in an unwed state for who would want her? Nobody, that's for sure. Coming around the back side of the sleek car, I couldn't help but notice Miss Taylor was in one of her big time snits. She was dead set on having her say, but Attorney Wilson Bagger got started first. I tuned the whole conversation out while continuing to explore the beauty of the Empire.

We had an old 1901 Model T Ford that Pa had traded a good plow horse for. Then with the help of a buddy, he added a pickup truck box on the back to haul supplies. But it didn't run half the time. We still used the horse hitched to the buckboard if the Model T wouldn't start, and we had to go to town for supplies. Truth is, I tried not to go with him on those trips. Some of my schoolmates gave me a hard time about our mode of transportation, and I had gotten into more fights over their making fun of our team of mules than for any other reason.

I was brought back to the present, and my head jerked around, when Ma loudly said, "No, you are dead wrong about Jeffrey! He's a good boy. I've raised him to be a Christian. We're in church every Sunday morning, and he listens hard to Brother Dan's messages. I won't hear another word against him!" I'd never heard Ma say words in such a harsh way. Her voice was shrill and shaking. I froze in place, staring as she whirled around, and with her apron pulled up over her face, ran into the house, slamming the screen door behind her so hard it rattled.

It must have stunned the three visitors as well 'cause they quickly decided their mission was finished and to take their leave. Pa shook hands with both of the men and attempted to assist Miss Taylor into the back of the car. She was too whopping mad to take any help and jerked away in a huff. I sidled around the car and stood close to Pa. I glanced over at him, but he wasn't looking at me. So I turned back to watch the back end of that incredible auto. The dust was swirling up from the tires in a thick cloud as they hurriedly headed back to town. I was thinking, *Bet it doesn't take them an hour to get there like it does me.*

I wasn't prepared for the racking sobs that carried out from the house to us. Pa didn't turn around but continued to watch the dust rising from the speeding car. Then he took off his hat and slapped it against his leg and turned toward me. He looked as sad as I felt, then he lit into me with a scolding like he never had before.

"I'm plumb ashamed of you, Jeff. Look what you've gone and done to your Ma. She defended you, but I swear you've got to where you don't think of nobody but yourself! Now, you're gonna be punished, but I don't know how until she settles down, and we can decide together." I was forced into a position of having to defend myself.

Trying to make the best of things, I reminded Pa, "Well, you said yourself you didn't see why I needed anymore schoolin' so I don't know what the big uproar is all about. I don't plan on going back there no more anyhow!"

"I'm right glad you decided that on your own, 'specially since they just said you won't be allowed to come back, ever!"

With that, he swung around and headed for the barn. Stomping along the dusty ground, he stirred up almost as much dust as the Empire. I knew what he said was true. They weren't goin' to let me back in school no matter what I said or did. I should have figured that out on my own since half the school board and ole Miss Taylor took the time to drive all the way out to our house. But it still shook me up; I hadn't thought that far ahead. What was I supposed to do now?

I stood there staring at his retreating back and looking up at the porch decided I'd better try to apologize to Ma and get one of them back on my side. She was still crying, and I just followed the sounds she was making.

She was sitting at the kitchen table, her elbows braced on the oilcloth, her head in her hands. She didn't look like she intended to stop bawling anytime soon. Even in her current state, she was a pretty woman. Everyone said so, and Ma wasn't young anymore. I figured she might be near as old as Miss Taylor, but you couldn't tell that by looking at her. Her hair was flaxen, and when the sun shone on it, the color was almost like gold and silver combined. No one in the whole county had hair as pretty as Ma's. It was falling down over her face now, hiding her eyes from me.

"Ma, I'm sorry, but it really wasn't my fault. Did you hear me? I said I was sorry."

Raising her head to look at me, I saw tears running unchecked down her cheeks. Her eyes were beet red and her face was all splotchy, and it made me feel plumb sorry 'cause deep down, I knew it was my fault. She shook her head and tried to stop the flow as she said, "Jeffrey, it's never you're fault. You just don't think things through. Why do you do these things without thinking?" She was staring at me, with her big blue eyes like she expected me to answer. But I didn't have an answer.

She was right though, I knew deep down that she was right as rain.

6

She had done her best to raise me right. Took me to church every Sunday, read me Bible stories when I was little until I knew them all by heart, and taught me manners that no one I knew used. She had always loved me, and she tried real hard to help me know the God she worshipped. I did have feelings about God once when I was younger.

I must have been in third grade when our preacher, Brother Dan, spoke of the love that God had for us. When he called for all to come forward and accept God's free gift, I walked down to the front and knelt down with the others. Ma was so happy she cried, along with several of the older ladies, but then they wept every time a lost soul found Jesus.

It felt awfully good for a while, but whenever I had to make a decision of some sort, I'd silence that voice inside me that whispered, "Wait, think this out," or "Don't do this, Jeffrey." Then I'd just jump headlong into it and wonder later why I didn't listen? But I couldn't seem to pay attention long enough for things to soak in deep enough to stay with me. Ma said I was "easily distracted" and was always on me to concentrate. Pa said I was just being a boy, and I'd grow out of it.

Besides, Pa seldom went to church with us, and he was a good man. Everyone said so. He was always the first to step up when a neighbor needed help, and he was the most honest man in the county.

I knew Ma hated it when he stayed home and we went without him. I got to where I felt guilty for always supporting Ma and felt the need to support him, too. Pa not going to church with us was one of the few things they argued about.

I could tell Ma wasn't going to let up weeping anytime soon, and she was so downtrodden I couldn't stand to look at her any longer. Turning around, I ran out of the kitchen and out the back door, slamming the screen door behind me. I headed down past the barn in a full run, hoping I wouldn't run into Pa. I couldn't bear the thought of Pa shaming me again, and I knew when he got back to the house and found Ma was still bawling, he was going to get even madder. Once I was far enough from the house, I slowed down to a walk, kicking up the red dust and watching the wind carry it away. I kept kicking it up until I got to the banks of the pond. Throwing myself down, I laid on my back staring up at the clouds wishing I could fly like the birds that darted above me. I watched the clouds floating overhead and wished I was anyone but me or anywhere but here.

Finally, I sat up and skipped rocks across the surface of the water and logged stones at the turtles that got too curious for their own good. I wasn't sure I hit any, but I scared quite a few. My stomach began to growl to alert me it was unhappy with me, too, and when I couldn't ignore it any longer, I got so hungry I had to go back. I wished I could pray. If I could, I'd promise God I'd be good from now on if he would only make Ma and Pa forgive me. But I figured He was probably as mad at me as they were, maybe as mad as ole Miss Taylor.

Daylight was running out, the last flush of sunset was waning, followed by the deep darkness of night that quickly fell. It was way past time for supper; I knew they would have been waiting for me for over an hour. Silently navigating my way back, I slunk slowly in the back door and peeked into the kitchen. They sat silently at the table with the cold food laid out in front of them.

Hesitantly, I said, "I'm sorry. I guess I sorta' lost track of the time."

Ma looked up at me and wearily rose to her feet. "Jeffrey, go wash your hands. I'll pour you some milk." Her voice was flat, and her shoulders were stooped over like she was defeated and too tired to keep fighting.

Pa wasn't even going to look at me, but I could tell by his posture he was madder than all get out. I quickly sat down and focused my attention on the bare plate in front of me. Not a word was spoken during the meal. I had lost my appetite between the back door and my kitchen chair. But not willing to draw any more attention to myself, I politely ate all that was put before me. Breaking the stifling silence, I whispered, "I'm finished." And pushing my chair back, quickly scooted out and headed to my room.

Tension was so thick in the house over the next couple of weeks that I spent time doing my chores without being prodded, and even hunted for things to do to help Pa. There was an unmistakable overtone of criticism passing between the two of them, and I was painfully aware it was all my fault. For the first time, I heard their voices raised in anger when I was in bed at night. I'd never heard them argue over anything but Pa staying home from church. I was becoming aware that what I had done was going to have long term consequences, and I didn't have an inkling of how to fix it.

Gradually, things got somewhat better, almost back to normal, and I made sure my behavior was exemplary. But an invisible wall had been raised between the two of them; we all ignored it, pretending like it wasn't there. It was as if the three of us were on shifting sand, powerless to do anything but try to stay steady and keep pretending that it was going to be all right.

They never decided what punishment was sufficient for my sin, and I avoided the subject like the plague. To say I was remorseful was too mild. I was filled with shame each day, not because I couldn't go back to school, but because I was afraid the rift between them was widening into a chasm that threatened their very lives together.

I had taken to staying home with Pa on Sundays. It just kind of became a habit, and Ma was mostly silent about it. I knew it was painful for her, but I was a man now so siding with Pa seemed the manly thing to do. She spent more and more of her time reading her Bible, and I knew she was lonely—lonely for the way things used to be before I went and did such a dumb thing. Her laughter was silent, and she stopped telling me stories about her childhood and how she had found Jesus when she was only six years old. Or maybe she sensed that I had quit listening when she spoke of God.

We got through the holidays and survived the long rough winter with the snow keeping us inside for two weeks right after Christmas. We didn't try to attend the Christmas celebration at the school house. It was the first time we had missed since I started school. Pa became so disgruntled during that time I tried to stay in my room to avoid him. We seemed to have become a family of malcontents all because I didn't want to get my knuckles rapped one afternoon. And yet the subject was never brought into the open. We sidestepped it like it was quicksand threatening to swallow us whole.

By spring, I had begun to think school hadn't been so bad after all. I kept pushing that thought to the back of my mind. I missed seeing what few friends I had, and the thought of not seeing Iris Ann Wilson was becoming almost painful. Iris Ann was the prettiest girl in school, not that she even knew my name, but I always thought someday I'd get the nerve to walk right up to her and say something like, "Well, Iris Ann, how are you doing?" And she would smile at me and wonder why she hadn't noticed me before. Thoughts like this are why I am having a hard time sleeping, and I know the chances of me ever seeing her again are less than zero.

Time hung heavy most days. There wasn't enough work to keep me and Pa both busy until later in the year when the crops were ready. Some days, I walked for miles until I couldn't stand to look at the same ole fields another time. And then there was the morning I woke up and knew I was going into town. I had hid out from every-body long enough. It wasn't like it was a plan or something; I just knew that was what I was going to do. I didn't say anything to Ma or Pa, but that had become how things were. Nobody said much, not even at the table when we ate our meals; sometimes, the silence grew so loud I wanted to start yellin' just to hear some noise.

I walked out the front door and started down the road toward town. If they noticed me leaving, they probably thought I was just out for another of my long walks. It's been seven months since that afternoon at the school. I try my best not to think on it, but we know

THE VOICES OF GABLE

that it changed us all. I wish I had a "do over". If I could just go back before I threw Miss Taylor down in my chair, I'd hold out the back of both hands and not even flinch when she slammed that ruler down on them. If I could do it over, I would, I swear!

Shaking my head to clear out the anger, I took a deep breath. There's a smell that carries on the wind in the spring. I don't rightly recall ever noticing it any other time. There's no way to describe it, but it's clean and almost like some kind of strange flower that you can't see. I was sniffing the air and walking the miles into town when that Empire Touring car passed me so fast it left me in a thick cloud of heavy dust that set my teeth on edge from the grit that filled my mouth. By the time the dust settled, the car was beyond my field of vision, and I felt the rage fill me up like a pitcher under the pump.

I cussed the air, the dirt on the road and everything else I could think of. I cussed out loud for so long my throat dried up, and deep down, I knew it was myself I was so mad at. It wasn't that I didn't want the banker to have that beautiful car, but I burned with resentment that I was walking and didn't see any possible way of changing my situation. How was I ever going to be able to earn enough money to buy my own car? Who would hire me with my reputation for acting out? No matter how loud I cussed, I couldn't drown out Ma's voice in my head, "Jeffrey, you will never be able to amount to anything without an education." She had long since stopped telling me this, but before I got expelled, she would remind me of it fairly often.

Sweat was burning my eyes and running down my face. I swiped my eyes on the sleeve of my shirt and tried to settle down. It was a big mess, that's for sure, and I couldn't think of anything to do to change it. Feeling lower than I had ever felt, I trudged the rest of the way into town. It wasn't a large town compared to some, I guess. But since it was the only town we had, and the only town I had ever been to, I didn't have much choice. I was wishing I could go someplace where no one knew who I was.

I kept my face downcast as I walked up and then down Main street. I didn't bother going into any of the stores since I didn't have so much as a thin dime on me. Now I was really mad at myself for not grabbing a dollar or two from my underwear drawer so I could have gotten me something to eat or drink. Ma was right. I just didn't think things through!

No one spoke to me, but I'm sure I didn't look like I wanted to visit, and the kids I knew were in school. The thought of school brought on another bout of anger, mostly at myself, but also at the whole world and everyone in it. I was an outcast by my own doing, but feeling isolated only increased my anger at the world in general. I was pure raging mad through and through.

I found my steps leading me to the familiar school house where the playground was empty, and I could hear the sounds of voices coming from inside. The teachers were talking about subjects, and I heard murmurs of the kids' replies. I could visualize Iris Ann sitting at her desk with her head down and writing in her notebook. I used to stare at her during class, just hoping she would sense me looking at her and turn around and see how crazy I was about her. She was a good student, and her folks had told everyone she would be the first in her family to attend college. She would too; she had a future, unlike me.

I stood on the outside, in front of the steps leading to the front door, gripping the top of the gate. It was the only opening in the fence that surrounded the school grounds. I had never felt so lost, and I was wishing I wasn't too old to cry. My stomach was tied up in knots, and I knew if I didn't get out of there in a hurry, I wouldn't be able to control myself, and I was gonna start bawling like a little kid. With my luck, Iris Ann would be coming out, and this time, she would get a good look at me, and I couldn't stand the thought of how much she would despise me.

It was then I realized I was standing beside the bicycle rack that held the bikes of the lucky kids who had one, and before I knew what I was going to do, I had gone and done it. I didn't decide to choose a particular one, or a particular color, I only wanted to get away from school and its bad memories and get home as fast as I could, and a bicycle would get me there in a hurry.

I grabbed the first one my hands settled on, and swinging my leg over the bar, I took off like a scared jackrabbit with a pack of dogs on my trail.

7

My lungs were screaming for air, and I was gasping like a fish out of water. I peddled like the devil himself was after me. Sweat was running down my back, and my legs were aching as I frantically rode pass the businesses dotting the only street out of town. On the street, a few people stopped and stared as I whizzed past them. No one yelled for me to stop. But I wouldn't have listened to them anyhow, no more than I was listening to that voice inside me begging me to turn around and return the bike where I got it.

I stopped my mind from thinking of what I was doing and just rode as fast as I could. My legs had stopped hurting, and I was breathing in and out and moving faster than I had ever moved before. As the town receded out of view, I slowed my pace a bit and quit looking over my shoulder for someone to catch up and grab me.

But then the voice was back, screaming inside my head, "What are you doing? Are you crazy? Take it back, take it back now!" But I was too scared to turn around and face the kids who, by now, would surely know that on top of everything else I had done, I had become a thief! And Iris Ann Wilson would hate the sight of me.

The closer I got to home, the slower I peddled. I was shaking uncontrollably and sobbing out loud like a newborn baby. What am I going to do? Oh, God, how am I going to explain this to Ma and Pa? Shoot, I can't explain it to myself! I don't know why I did such a stupid dumb thing. This time, they will hate me, for sure, and I can't blame them. They would be better off without me always messing up their lives. I'll run away, that's what. But where am I going to go? I've never been anywhere but around here where people know me. I don't know what to do. I can't think.

When I topped the knoll and saw our house, I got off and started walking with the bicycle by my side. Wiping my eyes and nose on my shirt sleeves, I tried to think things out, but it was like my mind had gotten buried in a thick pudding. I felt paralyzed with a choking fear. I didn't notice the fine spring day, or anything else now, only the sinking feeling that I had gone and done it again. And this time, I was in a heap of trouble.

I leaned the bike up against the maple tree in the front yard. I didn't bother to try to hide it, just left it in plain sight, a testament to the fact that I was now a common thief and would probably have to go to jail. Turning around, I walked slowly up the path, climbed the wooden steps to the porch, and stepped into the silent house. My heart was racing so hard I could hardly get a good breath, and it took me a spell to figure out nobody was home. I let out a big sigh of relief before the dread hit me in the pit of my stomach, they would be coming home sooner or later, and I was going to be in a mess of trouble.

The thought of facing them and telling them what I had done made me so sick I thought I was going to pass out. Ma's face kept appearing in front of me, reminding me of how hurt she was when I got expelled. How would she look at me now after what I've done? I paced around and around through the rooms I had grown up in, constantly peering out the windows for sight of them coming home. The panic was taking over, and I felt plumb feverish as I tried to slow down my breathing and get hold of myself. It seemed like hours had passed when I heard the sound of a car coming down the road. My heart dang near jumped out of my throat.

Hiding with my back pressed into the wall, I snuck a glance out the front window. Expecting to see Ma and Pa, my mouth fell open and fear coursed through me as I saw Sheriff Langer getting out of his car. Ducking back before he could see me, I stood shaking like a willow tree in a high wind. Oh god, oh god, what am I going to do?

"Jeffrey MacCreary, come on out here! It's Sheriff Langer, and we need to have a talk," he hollered. I was rooted to the floor and couldn't have moved if my life had depended on it. Suddenly, I felt an overpowering need for Ma and Pa to come home and make this go away.

"Jeffrey, I know you're in there, so come on out here like I told you!" This time, his voice was louder and he sounded madder. I took another quick peek and saw him with the bicycle in his arms, trying to load it in the trunk of his car.

I shut my eyes, and all of a sudden, like the shaking stopped, and my breath was coming in and out, deep and slow. Everything slowed down like I was under water, and I didn't seem to have control over my body. It just moved on its own without me having a say. Without thinking, I started walking toward his voice as if I was doing what he said. As I got to the front door, my arm reached up and lifted Pa's rifle down from its perch, and I stepped out onto the front porch.

I shut my mind down and didn't think of anything. I refused to listen to the voice that was screaming, *Don't! Don't, Don't!* I went deaf to any sounds and cradled the rifle in my hands. It didn't seem to weigh anything, like I wasn't really holding Pa's hunting rifle at all. Nothing was real, not the sight of him trying to stuff that bicycle into his trunk, not me staring at him from the porch.

Sheriff Langer turned toward me when he heard the screen door slam, and his eyes grew round with surprise and he opened his mouth to say something to me, but the rifle exploded and the bullet hit him almost dead center of his forehead.

I was as surprised as he was as I watched his head snap back and his body drop slowly to the ground. The trunk lid was still open, and the bicycle hung half in and half out of the trunk. The echoes of the rifle discharge faded, and the silence became deafening. Time stopped and stood still just like myself. That's how they found us when they spun into the yard.

They must have been getting close to the house and seen me come out on the porch, but I didn't see them or hear the car motor. Pa ran up on the porch, grabbed the rifle out of my hands, and threw it out into the yard. I do remember that Ma's screams echoed over and over, but not much else after I shot the sheriff. Things kept happening, people coming and going, and I just did what they told me. Lots of people came, the doctor who wasn't needed at all, most of the entire police force showed up and the local funeral parlor brought their big black hearse and took Sheriff Langer away with them.

The policemen shoved me roughly into the back of a squad car, and I watched as a couple of them finished putting the bicycle into the trunk of the sheriff's car and drove it away. I wanted to talk to Ma and Pa, but the policeman had locked me in, and when Pa started toward me, they took him by the arm and turned him around. It was like a horrible dream that's so scary you keep praying to wake up. I wanted to pray, but I was afraid to call God's attention to myself. He's probably as mad at me as everyone else is.

Most everybody was leaving except for a few neighbors and church members who came when they heard the news. Bad news travels a lot faster than good news. Even Brother Dan was here with his arm around Ma and talking quietly to her. People were gathered around the yard in little groups, talking earnestly among themselves. Some of the church women were patting Ma on the back and trying to console her. No one tried to come and speak to me, only glancing furtively my way now and then. Maybe they had been told to keep their distance, or maybe they couldn't bear to be near a thief and a murderer. I just kept staring at Ma and hoping she would look in my direction so I could somehow let her know I was sorry. I was real sorry!

Then the policeman got into the squad car, and turning it around in the yard, drove slowly down the road without a backward glance at me. Was it just this morning that I had set out on this very same road? No, couldn't have been. I felt years older than when I started out on my walk to town.

I turned around in the seat and looked back through the rear-view window and saw Pa helping Ma up the steps and into the house. If either one of them had looked back to see about me, I would have waved to them, but no one was looking at the retreating police car. I wondered how I was going to explain this to them when we were

THE VOICES OF GABLE

together again. We drove all the way into town and to the jailhouse without a single word being spoken.

Ma couldn't bear to see me in the jailhouse, so she didn't come. I missed her more than anything, but I couldn't blame her. Just seeing her for a minute would have helped. I wanted so badly to tell her how sorry I was. But she sent some of my favorite foods so I wouldn't waste away. Pa came twice a week and delivered the paper sacks of food, but he didn't stay long and mostly we sat with the table between us and tried to think of something to talk about without mentioning the fact that I was now a murderer. I just wanted the whole thing to be over.

None of the policemen had anything to say to me. I tried to tell a couple of them that I hadn't meant to harm Sheriff Langer, but they looked right through me like I wasn't even there. I was alone in my cell and scared of what was going to happen. Some cells had two or three prisoners in them, but they put me in the one farthest away from anyone. The days and weeks passed, and finally, a couple of months after the shooting, my trial began.

They gave me a lawyer who didn't seem to like me much, and I didn't see him but once before the trial began and that was right after my arrest. The first thing Lawyer Simpson asked me was, "Why in God's Holy name did you do such a hateful thing to such a fine man?" He wasn't too pleased with my answer.

"I guess I don't rightly know why I did it. I didn't even know it happened until it did."

"Jeffrey, why didn't you just go out and talk to Sheriff Langer? The worst thing that would have happened was he would have taken you into town, dressed you down, and turned you over to your parents. None of this needed to happen."

"I can't give you a reason 'cause I don't have any. I just didn't think."

"You didn't think? You didn't think! Well, because you didn't think, the town has lost a sheriff, two young'uns have lost their father, and a fine woman has lost her husband. That's a lot of misery because you didn't think!"

He gave me a disgusted look and turned on his heels and walked out of my cell. I didn't see him again until they brought me into the courtroom and even then, he tried not to have to look at me. I wanted to tell him I never meant for it to happen, but looking at his ramrod back, I knew he didn't want to hear anything I had to say. Nobody wanted to hear me speak.

They handcuffed my hands behind my back and lead me into the courtroom. My eyes searched the room for Ma and Pa, but only Pa was there, and he sat with his head down, and I could tell by the slump of his shoulders the weight of his sadness and the grief he was suffering. I wanted to die right there in that room for the trouble I had brought on them. Most everyone in town had shown up, and there wasn't one of them who were feeling anything for me but anger.

I guess the jury and the judge wanted me to have my wish 'cause after two days of everyone else having their say, they said I was guilty, which everyone already knew. The judge talked to me sternly before sentencing me to the electric chair. I started shaking when he said those words, like it was the most ordinary thing to say, like he said it most every day of the week.

When they took hold of me to lead me out of the courtroom, I tried to jerk away and get to Pa, but one of them hit me in the head with something, and I went out cold and didn't wake up until several hours later.

The next day, a jailer told me there was someone to see me, and he led me to a different room where there was a table with chairs on each side facing each other. I guess now that I had been declared a bonafide killer, this room was supposed to be more escape proof. Two armed guards stayed with us and remained standing silently by the door. Pa sat on one side, and they motioned for me to sit down across from him. I was so glad to see him I started bawling like a big baby, and I didn't care who heard me.

"Pa, I'm sorry, you tell them I'm sorry. I want to go home now."

"Jeffrey, son, don't you understand you won't be coming home again. You killed a man, and they're gonna put you in the electric chair for what you done. There ain't nothin' I can do for you. There ain't nothin' anyone can do to change that!"

Looking into his eyes, I knew the truth of what he said. I knew it all along but hearing Pa say it made it so. This wasn't going to be fixed. I wasn't going on with my life any more than Sheriff Langer was going on with his. And there was no one to blame but me.

I had quit crying, the tears had dried on my face. It was to be the last time I would cry for myself or for anything else. I reached across to take hold of Pa's hand, but the guard hollered out, "No touching!" So I had been touched by a loving hand for the last time as well.

"I haven't gotten to see Ma or talk to her. How is she? Why didn't she come with you?" I asked him with a plea in my voice. I had a hunger to see her so bad it was an ache in my heart. I felt just like she did when she spoke of missing her own mother.

He shook his head and said, "Your ma's sick, Jeffrey. She's been sick since that day. Some of the church ladies have been caring for her, but she's lost the will to live, and I can't seem to help her. The doctor says she's given up, and there's not much he can do."

The floor could have opened up and swallowed me, and I would have gladly gone with it. This was my fault. Ma was grieving herself to death because of me. A widow and two little young'un's were grieving because of what I did in a moment of stupidity. And looking at Pa, I saw how he had aged in these last months. I lost all fear of death at that moment. I would wait anxiously for it and welcome it to free me from this guilt. Nothing on this earth could give me peace or remove the memory of what I had done.

Pa rose up and started for the door. He still held his crumbled hat in his hand, the same hat that he had worn for as long as I could remember. "I'll try to come again before you get transferred to the penitentiary, Jeffrey, if your ma ain't worse. Good-bye, son."

"Good-bye, Pa." I said to his disappearing back. I had walked into that room as a little cry baby; I walked out a grown man, not any smarter, but no longer a youngun'. Pa didn't make it back to see me again, and they transferred me a few days later.

8

Penitentiary living was cold and mean, but it didn't matter. I existed only for the day when my life would cease. I didn't make friends, or even try, and because of what my crime was, no one bothered me. Time passed so slowly some days felt like a yearlong. I worked in the laundry from 7:00 a.m. to 5:00 p.m. six days a week. It wasn't too bad in the autumn and winter, but during the summer, it was stifling. Temperatures hovered around 110 degrees, and more than one convict ended up in the infirmary.

Finally, three years had passed since I had picked up Pa's rifle and stepped out onto our porch. After all this time, I still had no recollection of pulling that rifle trigger.

Three years, alone, without visitors, even on holidays when most of the prisoners had at least one visit from family or a girlfriend. I never let myself think about girls. The closest I had gotten to a girlfriend was pining for Iris Ann Wilson. I refused to let my mind wander and think on what might have been in my life "if" only I had thought things through. Being here, with no future, no friends must be a kind of hell. Maybe God will have mercy on me and give me credit for time served. Now wouldn't that be something?

Then one cold day, in the middle of November, they called me out and told me I had a visitor. My first and only visitor, except for Lawyer Simpson, who came once each year to let me know how things were going with my case. I was curious as they led me to the visitation room. I didn't figure it was the lawyer, as he had been here a couple of months before.

He was waiting for me on the other side of the glassed-in visitors' area. I hardly recognized the old man with silver hair and stooped shoulders. His hands moved constantly with tremors he couldn't control, and his eyes were bleak and lifeless. He had aged a lifetime since I had last seen him. I had heard from him, occasionally over the years, when someone would write for him, but I hadn't heard a word from Ma in all this time.

"Pa, are you all right?" my voice choked up at the sight of him.

He nodded his head and shakily told me, "I had to come see you face to face, I didn't want to let you know in a letter that someone else would have had to write. Your ma died a week ago, son. I tried to get them to let you out to come to her funeral, but they said no."

The room began to spin, and a dark hole was opening up in front of me. Shaking my head to clear it, I tried to speak through the knot in my throat, it took me several tries. "Thanks for coming, Pa. I'm so sorry. I know this is all my fault." He avoided looking at me and didn't answer me or try to make me feel better. He never could tell a lie.

"Did any of her people come?"

"No, they was notified, but I never heard from any of them. She had a real hard time, Jeff, but she's at peace now, and I have found my own way to God. I'll join her when it's my time. I know that will please her. Is there anything I can do for you, son?"

"No, Pa, no, there's nothing I need. And I don't want you to come here again. It's too long a trip for you, and I'm fine. I'm not afraid. Maybe you and Ma's God will be able to forgive me someday. You go on home now Pa, and... I love you."

We stared at each other for the longest time before he turned, and I watched him shuffle in his old man's gait through the exit door. Watching his back, as he went out, I realized that very soon I would be an orphan; I would be nobody's child. It was the loneliest feeling in the world and knowing the electric chair would be the tool that would end this misery, I longed for the peace it would bring.

I wanted those last words to Pa to be my last words so I never uttered another word to anyone, not even to the preacher who came to talk and comfort me. I remained silent even as they walked me to the death room two years after Pa's visit.

They shaved my head the day I was to be executed, but I wasn't allowed to have a mirror so I couldn't see myself. Then they took my shoes and socks so I would walk to the chamber barefooted. Several of the jailers and even the warden escorted me down the long hallway. The preacher stayed by my side though I had never responded to anything he said since the day Pa left. I knew that what I had done was unforgivable and that included forgiveness from God Almighty, so there was no use pretending otherwise.

The other prisoners on death row hollered and yelled as we walked past them. I wasn't friends with any of them, but I guess it made them feel better. It was a long walk to the strange little room with tall glass windows on all sides and a big ugly chair sitting in the middle of it. There were all kinds of leather straps that would bind me for my last minutes on this earth. The wall of glass windows let the visitors seated in rows in front of me watch me take my last breaths on this earth. I avoided looking directly at any of them.

I began to shake when they shoved me down onto the hardness of the chair and started strapping me in, not because I was afraid, but it seemed to be so cold in there. I'd never felt such bone chilling cold. No one spoke as they placed the straps around my body. The concrete floor felt like ice to my bare feet. The last thing they did was place this metal crown on top of my head. Like a flash of light, I could see the crown of thorns being smashed down on Jesus's head, and for some strange reason, it struck me as funny that me and Jesus both had us a crown at our ends.

I began to laugh and looking up at the witnesses saw the unbelieving shock on their faces. It was the last memory I have of being alive.

I met my fate with a certain eagerness. "The youngest man to be executed in the state of Oklahoma", that's how the papers described me over and over. I was a month shy of being twenty-two years old.

I'm thinking that's quite an epitaph, but I know it would have pained Ma something fierce.

And now I remain in a kind of prison. This is not at all what I expected. To be honest, I don't know what I expected but for sure it was not this.

Time doesn't matter here. Not like it did when I was alive. I think it's been a long time since I first came here, but I've lost count of the seasons that have passed. There's nothing to do but relive over and over what I did and think about what I shoulda' done.

These grounds are surrounded by a rock fence, like a short fortress, that keeps me trapped inside, and I see no one unless people come to bury a loved one. Then the autos arrive and turn in through the double gates, leaving the dusty road that runs in front of the cemetery. When the rains don't come, the red dust settles over the tombstones, and when the rains wash them clean, the ruts in the road make it hard for the long black hearse to maneuver to the freshly dug graves.

Ma and Pa are buried here, and there is a small marker with my name on it, but I must not be buried or I wouldn't be forever stranded in this strange place, would I? I just amble around these grounds and try to forget how I wasted my life. But that's not possible because the memories haunt me day in and day out.

There's a small church that stands in the corner, up close to the road. It's built from the same sandstone as the fence. This land is full of sandstone. It had kept Pa and me busy pulling them out to plow and plant new ground. They don't look like much but they're solid. I don't know how long this little church has been standing, but it'll last for a long time. Sometimes, I'll sit in one of the pews and pretend I'm back with Ma and try to remember the sound of her voice as she sang along with the hymns, her hair that was the color of gold and silver mixed when the sun shone on it, all the things that bring her close to me again. An old black piano stands in one corner, and occasionally, when they hold a funeral here, I can hear the music and remember the hymns from so long ago.

I miss her… all the time. Those times when we sat side by side on a wooden pew and listened to the preacher speak of God and how much he loved us were the best times I can remember.

I feel the presence of others around me. I know they are here, but they are invisible to me, and I guess I am to them as well.

The guilt never goes away; it still weighs heavy and fills me with such sorrow. I continue to grieve, but there are no tears, only this strange feeling of waiting—waiting for something or someone, I don't know which.

Aaron stood beside Jeffrey listening to the sound of the suffering in his soul. The demons that tormented his charge never let up, and though Aaron was the mightiest of the guardian angels, standing over seven feet tall and seasoned from his many battles since the beginning of time, he was powerless to use force until given a sign from the Master.

His cobalt eyes flashed ominously as the stench of the sulfurous demons came too near his proximity. Seeing the look of anger on his chiseled features was enough to scatter some of the lowliest demons. Knowing he was reaching the end of his patience, Aaron made the decision to visit his leader, the archangel Michael, for much needed direction. The enormous wings spread out from his massive back and the powerful thrust, as he rose into the heavens, caused the trees to bend in the sudden gust of wind that howled across Gable Cemetery.

Aaron soared into the heavens, straight up; his powerful wings barely felt the effort. His mind so full of thoughts of his charge he failed to notice the magnificent beauty that surrounded him. Arriving before the great archangel, Michael, he was meekly subservient in the presence of his mentor and leader.

"It is good to see you again, Aaron." Michael greeted him warmly as always.

"Thank you, Michael. I sorely needed to spend some time with you, for I am in need of your guidance now, as never before. Barael told me of his visit with you and that your word was for us to continue to be patient. I want to know, I need to know, when will we be given authority over the demons again?"

Sighing heavily, Michael motioned for Aaron to sit down with him. "Our visit will take a while, and it is easier on my neck if you are sitting." Michael was obviously in good humor, and Aaron felt the tension drain away and returned the smile.

"Aaron, tell me about this current charge of yours and what you think of him. You have always given your reports on him, but now I want to know what this charge means to you."

Hesitating for a few moments to gather his thoughts, he said, "Jeffrey is a strange one. There is no malice in him. He deeply regrets the sins he committed. He is capable of great love, but he reacted without thought and the evil one leaped on this flaw and used his legions of demons to influence and goad Jeffrey into the ghastly decisions he foolishly made."

Michael nodded his head in agreement. "I see, as usual, you are very astute in your assessment. Now, you may ask me your questions and I shall try to explain as best I can."

"Why can't we eliminate the vile demons and set our charges free to see the Master's great love for them, and His mercy and grace?" Aaron's face was animated with intensity.

"Ah, yes, that would be a simple solution, wouldn't it? However, the Master has given His human children something called 'free will', and if you take away all of their options or choices, then they become as robots, and if that is what the Master longed for, then the Son died for no reason. They must be free to choose. It is because of His great love for them that these are being given another opportunity before they stand before Him. And you, and Barael, and the others are watching over them to see that things are not taken too far. The time will come when you will be set free, but for now, continue as you have been. Do you understand, Aaron?"

Looking somewhat chastised, Aaron nodded his head in acknowledgment. He was not only a mighty warrior but well known for his intelligence and leadership.

"I think I understand. It is a complicated business guarding these flawed humans, but it is an honor to guard the Master's loved ones. But, I tell you, I will look forward to the day when we can annihilate these demonic fiends. Their stench is almost more than I can bear!"

Michael rose and motioned to Aaron that their meeting was over. "I know it is a most difficult time, but changes are coming. The time is near when all of God's angels will be released. Be patient, my friend. It is coming quickly."

Feeling much relieved, Aaron spread out his massive wings and dove straight down through the layers of the universe into the atmosphere of Earth and landed stealthily beside Jeffrey, who did not notice the presence of his heavenly guardian. But then, he had never been aware of this powerful presence.

A lone dog stood outside the stone wall that surrounded the cemetery, his head rose upward, and his black nose sniffed the air. He was attuned to the sounds coming from within the grounds, but it was the smell that caused him to growl low in his throat, the shackles along his back raised, and he began to back up, putting distance between himself and whatever it was inside the grounds.

Aaron found that animals always knew when a demon was near, but humans did not seem to have that ability. "Too bad, for the vulgar repugnant aroma that arises from their loathsome bodies could be an alarm for God's chosen ones. Then they would be alerted to call upon their Heavenly Father and release the power of their guardian angels to deal with the abominable ones." He spoke out loud and Barael, who was standing nearby, heard his words but remained silent as the two warriors stood guard over their charges.

PART 3

1969

"And then there were three."

9

The clouds were thick and roiling. It would be dark soon and the lawmen, medical personnel, press, and bystanders were all of like mind, all hoping the storm would hold off for a little longer. This was nasty business they wished was over or had never begun. The sound of distant thunder announced it was coming and coming soon.

The divers had been under for a long time, and if they didn't find something quickly, they would have to be called up and the search continued tomorrow. Max Webster stood on the rocky shore at a distance from the rest. Max was from a long line of officers serving the OHP (Oklahoma Highway Patrol) dating back almost to the beginning when the force was created in 1937.

During the last twenty-nine years, only once was there a time when his family was not represented on the distinguished patrol. For a time, the Websters produced nothing but girls, and none of them felt the desire to follow the family tradition nor would they have been allowed to serve as officers.

Then Max's independent mother divorced his absentee father, reclaimed her maiden name, changed her children's last names to match hers, and the OHP was back in the family business. Max was the youngest son, raised on his grandfather's stories of serving in the OHP, and there was never a doubt in his mind what he would become.

He had been on duty for almost eighteen years, climbing the ladder of responsibility until reaching his current status, deputy chief, one of three under the Chief of Patrol. His jurisdiction covered all of zone six. He and his troopers were stretched thin throughout the network of turnpikes that zigzagged across the landlocked state, formerly known as Indian Territory.

He wasn't required to be here, but every time the dive team was called out, Deputy Chief Webster appeared on site, and no one questioned his motives. He always prayed for a miracle on his way to these sites, and occasionally, his prayers were answered, although they were a rarity.

He tried not to think on his reasons for being drawn to the water rescues, but the fact was Deputy Chief Max Webster was deathly afraid of water. To his way of thinking, drowning was at the top of the list of worst ways to die, and he had seen most of the ways that could turn a human being into a corpse. Max knew that, over the years, he had seen more than his share of death, but being here was his way of facing down that deep rooted fear he kept hidden from everyone, including his wife.

"Sir!" the young officer stood beside him and was staring intently at Max's face.

Shaking himself out of his reverie, he confronted the scene and replied, "What is it?"

"They've found it, sir. We have the tow truck moving into position now. As soon as the divers get the cable hooked to the car, it shouldn't take long to bring it up."

Max didn't bother to reply, just shook his head in assent. There would not be a miracle on this day. The car had been submerged for too long. Witnesses had seen the car swerve from one side of the road to the other, flip over the guard rail, roll down the steep slope, and finally, sail airborne into the depths of the farm pond.

It was a beauty of a pond, unusually large for this area, and the kind that every farmer or rancher envied. Almost big enough to be called a lake, deep enough for a boat to troll. It was surrounded on three sides by a variety of trees, so if you were fishing, you could always find a shady spot in which to set up. Just the kind of place

Max dreamed of when thinking of retirement, but not this pond. It had been spoiled by the tragedy on this day, and he wouldn't be coming around here again. "Darn shame, too," Max sighed under his breath.

The first drops of rain were beginning to fall, causing the bystanders to make a run for the security of their automobiles. The wind had picked up, and Max knew if they didn't get the car up and onto the bank soon, the force of the wind was going to cause havoc for the tow truck driver. Even worse, this storm was coming in from the north, and the driving rain was quickly turning into stinging sleet. Lowering his head, Max silently asked his God for just a little more time... the last thing he wanted to do was notify the next of kin that their loved ones spent this miserable night submerged in the dark water.

Concerned about the worsening weather, Max called over the trooper in charge and suggested, "If the witnesses have given their statements, you may want to release them to head for home. Let's try to clear out some of these cars and trucks along the roadway." Trooper Jamison was more than happy to follow his leader's advice and quickly set about dispersing the crowd. Only a few die-hards hung around hoping to see how this would play out.

The lone TV crew stood patiently at a distance, and Max had to feel sorry for them, especially the attractive young reporter, who definitely had not watched her local weatherman's prediction for this front coming through. She was huddled over; pulling her light suit jacket tight around her and her once perfect hair was now hanging limply about her face. She looked like a kitten soaked to the skin. The cameraman was trying to protect his equipment from the driving wind and sleet, and the young driver, who looked like he wasn't old enough to shave let alone drive, was hunkered down against their van trying to protect himself as well. Neither man seemed to notice the lovely young woman.

There were no sounds except the sleet pelting around them and the whirl of the gears drawing the cable as the submerged automobile began to rise from beneath the murky water. All eyes were glued to the scene in front of them.

The swishing sound was distinct as the depths of the pond gave up its hostage. There was a strong suction as the front end of the automobile rose above the dark water. You could faintly make out the make and model of the cream and tan '57 Ford Fairlane. Algae and debris dripped across the bank as the car was lowered onto the ground. Water was escaping around all four sides of the ruined Fairlane, and the figure of the lone occupant gradually came into view as the troopers and doctor from the medical examiner's office crowded around it.

Max stood at his customary distance not needing to view the aftermath. He was relieved when it was reported there was only one person in the car, feeling fortunate they had somehow dodged a bullet. Silently, he gave thanks to his God that an entire family had not been in the ill-fated automobile.

The sleet was heavier now and mixed with snow. The worsening conditions made it difficult to complete the task at hand. The TV crew had finished their news coverage, giving up on getting good visual footage, and made a dash for the warmth of their vehicle. Max pulled his heavy, hooded coat tighter around his body, trying to keep the blasting wind from knocking him over. Thinking of his warm house and his wife, Rebecca, waiting for him with the hot strong coffee he preferred, it was all he could do not to bolt for his own vehicle.

Trooper Jamison made his way over to stand in front of Max and reported, "Looks like the victim was DUI. We found two empty bottles and another half empty bottle of scotch. If he drank it all today, then he may have passed out and probably never knew when he hit the water."

Max had to yell to be heard above the wind, "Thanks, Jamison. I'll head out and look at your full report in the morning. Good job." With that, he turned and climbing into the freezing confines of his car, started the motor and let it run a bit before pulling back onto the roadway.

10

Jack Simmons was in a state of absolute confusion. He was some-what aware that the car rising above the water was his twelve-year-old Ford, but the last thing he remembered was trying to keep his eyes open and not run off the roadway. Watching the horrific scene play out before him, he was stunned to see himself pulled from the water soaked car and laid out on a stretcher. Heavy, wet snow was now falling, and it was difficult to see through the blizzard although he was strangely aware that the cold or wind had no effect on him.

"What's happening? I don't understand. Why don't you answer me!" he shouted at the milling figures surrounding him.

The crowd had gathered in several small groups, staying close together to keep from being buffeted by the driving wind and snow. But no one heard Jack Simmons's pleas, nor saw the stricken man in their midst.

"Someone tell me what's going on! Oh god, this isn't right!"

Frantic in his confusion, he struggled to make sense of the bizarre happenings. "This is a nightmare. That has to be it. I'm dreaming, and I just need to wake up." He laughed out loud, but no one heard his nervous laughter.

"Boy, what a dream this is. I may just have to let up on the booze when I wake up from this." Jack chuckled nervously. But a sinking feeling was starting to grow inside him, which quickly grew stronger. His enigmatic situation was becoming more ominous as he watched a dark hearse drive into the proximity, and the solemn crowd stepped aside, making room for them to get to his body.

His body—his badly injured, lifeless body—was laid on the stretcher, and Jack felt himself standing on a precipice as he began to fall into the deep chasm, and then there was nothing.

Orion was a silent presence, remaining close to his charge. The circumstances of his charge's earthly demise came as no surprise to him. The only curious thing was that it had not happened many years before.

Orion, like Barael and Aaron, was a powerful angel. These three proven warriors were utilized repeatedly throughout the ages by the great archangel Michael for the most difficult assignments. They were held in high esteem by all the host of heaven. Michael always had full authority, directly from the throne, and therefore, his orders were never questioned by the legions of angels under his command. Over the eons of time, as he selected and placed the warriors where he chose, not one would have dreamed of undermining his respected leader.

But it was a bit unusual for these three mighty angels to take on the mundane task of watching over charges. And these assignments were usually deemed completed when charges left the earth and their lives upon it were finished. But not this time.

Voices were whispering throughout the heavenly realms over this most unusual occurrence, but no one raised a question to Michael and certainly not before the throne.

Jack, unaware of the heavenly being at his side, suddenly found himself in a small cemetery without knowledge of how he had gotten there. Staring at his surroundings, the thought that he had been here before struck him with force. But he was too confused to think it out.

There were pieces, like a puzzle, floating in a jumbled mass inside his head until he was in a totally baffled state.

He had had this same reaction on many occasions when he awoke from a bender of drinking himself into oblivion. He had awakened to strange, unfamiliar surroundings not knowing where he was, or how he had gotten there. But this was different. This time, he was stone-cold sober. More sober than he could remember being in many, many years, and the desire for a drink was almost overpowering.

"Hey, anybody here?" he called out and then listened carefully as if fully expecting someone to answer. There was only the sound of the ferocious wind blowing what few leaves remained on the old blackjack trees. Even with the wind howling, there was an eerie silence surrounding him for there were no human voices. Jack started to laugh when it hit him that he would have given almost anything to hear the sound of a television muffled in some room.

Moving a few feet to his left, he found that he could move his body just fine, although it was quite different than when he was alive.

"That's it, I'm not alive, am I?" he asked the empty space around him. "Now wait a minute, if I'm dead, then how can I be in this place and be able to walk around as I choose?" Jack was becoming comfortable conversing with himself. Strangely, he did not feel afraid, only a vague apprehension, as he began to cautiously explore his surroundings.

The blizzard was blowing the snow around him, and there were mounds of snow piling up against the headstones. Dotted here and there were large grave markers indicating the bodies laid to rest beneath them were of some affluence. But most were small in stature, and some were already covered in the drifting snow.

As he roamed in and out among the headstones, Jack was struck by the gravity of his situation. The sense of being smothered was overcoming him, he felt haunted by a deep sense of homelessness, and loneliness was swiftly growing inside him like a malevolent cancer. At this thought, he laughed somewhat hysterically, and thought to himself, *That's one good thing about being dead, cancer doesn't scare me anymore.* But the darkness of his situation was setting in, and for the first time, Jack was frightened... deep down terrified out of his mind.

And the restless wind continued to blow over the tiny cemetery located in the small county of Lincoln in the state of Oklahoma. The state, too, was small, at least when compared to its southern neighbor, Texas. There was nothing special that stood out about the location or the souls that rested here, but high above the firmament, up into the heavens, all the way up to the throne, things were happening, and a plan had been set in motion. A plan that had been hidden since before the beginning of time.

11

For Jack, time no longer had the same meaning it had when he was alive. The watch that belonged to his grandfather no longer circled his left wrist. He was not wearing the familiar jewelry he had grown accustomed to over the years, not even the wedding ring he had refused to take off.

"How long have I been here, I wonder?" He walked incessantly throughout the cemetery grounds as his mind raced. He was filled with unanswered questions.

"This must be a kind of hell, the kind of hell where loneliness drives you insane. I'm trapped with my own troubling thoughts, and right now, I'm not too pleased with having myself as a companion. I want someone to talk to, anyone, even if they read me the riot act. I might actually listen this time! I know what I want, I want a *do over*. Come on! Whoever's in charge here, you could let me have that one little wish, can't you? And these blasted memories keep running through my head no matter how hard I try to shut them down. They're constantly attacking me as if tormenting me to death, but that's funny because I'm already dead."

Jack could find no peace as his thoughts continued. The voice inside my head is louder than ever. I spent my whole life trying to ignore that small voice inside of me. Every time I wanted to get wild and have some fun, the voice would get louder and louder. It wasn't a male voice, but it wasn't female either, it still isn't. When I was alive, I learned that if I drank enough, I could drown it out.

He laughed out loud. "Ironic, isn't it? I had to drown to get here, and the voice is still with me. I spent the biggest part of my life ignoring it by drinking myself into oblivion, and now the voice is constantly speaking inside my head. The liquor was like an off and on switch, only it stayed in the off position enabling me to blot out the voice. Now, it's constantly reminding me of what I did with my life. It plays out like a bad B movie, and I can't get it to stop."

The seasons are coming and going. I still don't understand why I'm here. Is this the hell the preacher used to scare me with? Eternity, whew… is that what this is going to be? If the voice would shut up, I wouldn't be filled with such melancholy. I'd go crazy if I could.

My thoughts keep going back to my mother now. God, I haven't let myself think of her since I took my first drink. Alcohol was a double-edged sword, wiping out memories of her and silencing the voice that condemned every decision I made. Now she is in my thoughts constantly, and sometimes, her memory brings me a sort of peace, at least the early memories. I remember her laughter the most. The way she would toss her head, flinging her long red hair back, and when she laughed, I couldn't keep from giggling along with her. It didn't matter that I was too young to know why she was laughing, we would laugh until she would grab me up and hug me so tight I could barely breathe. I loved the smell of her, not any spray from the dime store, but her own unique smell."

"Granny and Papa only had one child, and she couldn't have been more different from them. Laughing and bubbly, never serious, and full of mischief, she kept them in a constant state of worry over what she might do next. They dragged her to every church service and prayed that some of it would rub off on her. Even as a young child, she was filled with a recalcitrant nature that the passage of time could not dilute."

When she finished high school at the early age of sixteen, she packed her few belongings in one suitcase and left in the middle of the night without a word to anyone. They wouldn't see or hear from her again until late August, four years later, when she stood on their front porch with her one suitcase and me hanging on her hip. We must have been quite a shock to two old people who had given up ever seeing their child again. Of course, peace went out the back door when we arrived at the front. And again, they jointly prayed for divine intervention.

News of our arrival spread like wildfire throughout the small town. Momma was hard to ignore, and most of the men in the community went out of their way to stumble across her path. Most women avoided her presence.

I guess one of the agreements to our staying with Papa and Granny was that we both attend church when they did, so I was as familiar with a sanctuary as I was my own bedroom. I had a pretty fair voice, and singing in the choir was something my grandparents encouraged. The females of the congregation never invited my mother to sing with them even though she had a beautiful voice. When she felt real devilish, you could hear her above the entire choir.

For me, in the early years, there was the feeling of peace and safety inside the walls of the church and inside the house that Papa and Granny provided for us. I can't really remember what it was like before we came home to them, but knowing Momma, I doubt if peaceful entered into our lives. I must have been around three when we invaded their quiet home, and no matter what they must have thought, they opened their hearts to us.

I was six years old when they put their collective foot down. "Naomi, this has gone on long enough. We've been patient, but its past time for you to settle down, get to work, and take on your fair share!" This time, Papa was adamant.

Granny had the final word, and it was a doozie. "And don't think for one minute that you will be taking Jack with you. He stays with us! So make up your mind. I'm not getting any younger. Either you start acting responsibly or you leave… alone. Those are your choices."

So my mother found a job as a secretary at the local feed store and within three months received a proposal of marriage from a local rancher twice her age who, before running into her, had been a confirmed bachelor. The local women were put out something fierce that she had nabbed him, but Naomi Simmons became Naomi Guiderian, and there was nothing to be done about it. There wasn't a widow around that could compare to Momma.

As we packed our bags and prepared to move to Thomas Guiderian's place, Granny and Papa stood on the porch waiting for us as we came out. Grabbing me in a long hug, Granny whispered to me, "Jack, we'll come by every Sunday and take you to church with us. You remember that Jesus loves you, and He will always be with you." I heard her, but I wiggled free without answering, anxious to get on to this new adventure.

My new stepfather preferred to be called Thomas, not Tom, and it seemed the only thing we had in common was that we both adored my mother. He couldn't seem to get enough of her, always following her around. He was constantly thinking up excuses to come into the house throughout the day. His consistent hovering became a nuisance to her, and she took to making faces at him behind his back, but so I could see. I would go into peals of laughter, which irked Thomas and didn't do my standing with him any good.

"Jack, it's time for you to start learning about being a rancher. After all, you're going to be the oldest young'un around here when your mother and I start a family of our own."

Thomas made this announcement at the breakfast table, and Mom was as astonished as I was, but after thinking it over, she shrewdly decided it might be a very good idea. So I began my education to be a rancher. Ole Thomas used the time he kept me busy to slip into the house and pester Mom.

I remember being happy, with school, ranching, and going to church with my grandparents on Sundays. Thomas and I reached a silent agreement, we tolerated each other and both loved the same woman.

I had just turned nine when one Sunday I walked down the center aisle and dedicated my life to Christ. I meant it, too. With all my young heart, I loved Jesus, as the hymn said, "Because He first loved me." And promptly that afternoon, half the church followed us down to the farm pond on Granny and Papa's place and watched me be baptized by Brother James. Even Mom and Thomas came along to watch. I felt changed somehow, different, like there was someone else along with me, and that's when the voice began.

When school started, I rode the bus to and from each day. I loved school, and it turned out I was a pretty good athlete. I was the first one picked for ballgames during recess. I never got to play any games after school because the school buses were always lined up right outside the front door, waiting for us farm kids.

A couple of months into the school term, Mom surprised me when she took to picking me up from school each day instead of having me ride the school bus home. When Thomas complained, she told him, "It's only because this way, he can get home quicker and get to his chores, honey." He couldn't think of any reason to make her stop picking me up so I quit riding the big yellow bus.

And most days that was true, on other days we would make a detour. She would stop at the local Dairy Queen and get me a large cone dipped in hot fudge. Then we would stop at a house a few miles from town and she would tell me, "Jack darlin', you wait right here for me. I'll be out in a while. Now you wait for me, hear?"

I didn't mind. I always had a book to read or homework to get done. When she would come out, she would pat her hair into place and smile one of her perfect smiles and ask, "Honey, did I make you wait too long?" No, she couldn't do anything wrong as far as I was concerned, and I never questioned her about why we were stopping at the same house a couple of times a week. She always reminded me that it would be best if we didn't mention going to the Dairy Queen or the time she spent at the house to Thomas, which was fine with me. Thomas and I didn't spend time talking about anything but farm work.

But things at home were changing. There was a growing tension in the air almost thick enough to split. I didn't know what to think about it, but I kept wishing things would go back to the way they were.

One night, I heard them quarrelling and picked up on a couple of things they were saying, "Oh, Thomas, you're imagining things. You know I love you, honey." And Thomas's voice replied, "Then why are there no other children in this house, Naomi? We should have had two or three by now. I know you are able because of Jack."

"Because of Jack," that's what he said. I caught my breath. Then this was my fault! But I didn't know what I might have done. I lay awake worrying on it long after they had ceased their arguing and fallen asleep. A sense of uneasiness hung over me after that, and as time went on, it grew into a fearful darkness that overshadowed all of us.

I tried to make Thomas like me. I did my chores without being told and followed him around like one of the barn cats after a milk pail. It got to where we could talk as long as the subject was the farm. I never brought Mom up in our conversations, and he never spoke of her to me. As long as we were outside, the pall that hung over us dissipated, but once the three of us were inside the house together, it hung over us like a dark cloud, and Mom's laughter had ceased altogether.

I didn't tell Granny and Papa anything, about what was happening, when they picked me up on Sunday mornings. But they must have known something was wrong because sometimes Granny questioned me until Papa told her to hush up, and they would look at each other with a strange expression on their faces.

12

It was spittin' rain that afternoon when she again picked me up from school. This was our last day before Christmas break, and I was excited at not having school for three whole weeks. I'd turned ten just before Thanksgiving and had gotten everything I asked for. Granny and Papa got me a red bicycle, and Thomas and Mom relented and let me have the .22 rifle I had been begging for. I had been chosen to be Joseph in the church play, and we were starting practice that very evening. For a little while, I had forgotten the feeling of a dark happening coming on us.

I dumped all my junk in the back seat and climbed into the passenger seat beside her. She seemed nervous, unlike her usual carefree self. Glancing over her shoulder, she pulled away from the school and turning to me said, "Jack, we need to make one stop on our way home. I have to see someone about something."

"Okay, but don't forget I have to be at the church by six o'clock." I reminded her. She didn't answer, but her fingers were clutching the steering wheel so tight her knuckles were white. I began to feel apprehension building up, and when she remained quiet as we drove along, my stomach started to churn. I kept stealing glances at her, but she was concentrating on the road and never looked at me.

It was an unfamiliar road we were on, all dirt and barely wide enough for two cars to pass each other. I didn't recognize anything, and after she made several turns, I was completely lost. The raindrops were starting to turn to snowflakes, and although she cranked the heater up on high to warm us, I felt chilled to the bone.

She finally came to a stop in the middle of nowhere, and we sat there on the side of the little dirt road without speaking, the car idling silently, and waited for whatever disaster was coming for us.

It came in a dark green pickup with white lettering on the side of the doors announcing it belonged to A-Z Contractors. Pulling up alongside of us, there was no movement for a long time. My heart was beating so fast I thought it would jump out of my chest.

Looking at Mom, as she stared out her window without moving, I said loudly, "We need to go. Please, Mom, let's get out of here! Listen to me, let's go!" I was pleading with her. But she didn't turn around or acknowledge she had even heard me.

I was having trouble breathing, and I could see Mom was trembling. "Hush, Jack," she said quietly without looking at me. Then the door of the pickup opened, and a man walked around in front of it and came up to us. He laid his hands on the top of the car and leaned down to be face to face with her. As she rolled down her side window, I got a good look at him. He was big and dark skinned with silver hair at his temples, and he was not happy when he saw me.

"What did you have to go and bring the kid for?" he asked her through clenched teeth. His jaw was rigid, and his eye's narrowed to slits.

"Don't get upset, Jimmy, there were no buses running today, and I couldn't leave him at the schoolhouse." There was a pleading sound to her voice like a little child asking for another chance. I looked at her and wondered why she lied to this man. Of course, the buses were running or else how would all the kids get home?

"Never mind, Naomi, I want an answer now. I told you I wasn't waiting any longer for you to decide!" His voice was low and menacing. He was staring intently at her like nothing else in the world existed. My body began to shake.

"Jimmy, sweetheart, I need more time, please. This is a big decision, and I have Jack here to think about. After Christmas, I'll decide, I promise!" Her voice was full of emotion, and there was a sense of urgency in the sound of her vow.

But I saw the look on his face change.

"No, not again, I've waited a year for you to leave him. I told you I wouldn't give you up, and no one else is going to have you!" He was screaming as he pulled a pistol from his jacket pocket, and I don't think he heard my screams as the gun went off and her head flew backward. Blood splattered across my face, and all I could hear were my screams ricocheting throughout the car.

The man jumped back, staring at the blood flowing from her head, and turning around, he stumbled to his pickup, revved the engine, and spun out leaving us alone on the empty road. Alone, lost, and unable to move, I let her blood dry on my face as if removing it would have wiped her out as well. Her eyes were open, and I wanted so bad to close them, but I was terrified that if I moved, I would explode into tiny pieces.

I must have gone into shock then because I have no memory of the hours I spent in the deathly silent car throughout the night. The next morning, when the heavy fog had lifted and the sun had risen above the tree line, the police found us. I was still sitting in the front seat beside my mother's body. The car had long since run out of gas, and it was frigid cold inside. I couldn't control my shaking, and I couldn't remember how to speak. It was all so strange.

Granny and Papa came to the hospital stunned and grieving. They had aged a generation since I had last seen them. Granny's tears refused to stop flowing, and Papa was pale as a ghost. I wanted to comfort them, but words wouldn't come out, and all I could do was let her wrap me in her arms and curl up like a baby. After a few hours, they loaded me up and took me back to their place. The police followed us hoping once I was in a safe familiar place, I could tell them what happened.

It took several days and when I did come to myself, I gave them the man's name and description, but they didn't really need my story. Jimmy had driven into town and sitting in front of the drugstore, with a half empty bottle of whisky beside him, had shot himself with the same gun he used to kill my mother. Evidently, their affair was not as secret as Mom had thought. It didn't take long for the police to piece it together, and after I told them my story, they wrapped it up quickly.

There was a private service at the gravesite. Right here in Gable Cemetery, no wonder this place seemed so familiar when I got here. It was snowing and cold the day she was buried, just like it was when I came here. They buried me beside her in the family plot along with Granny and Papa. I wonder if Sue Ann was the instigator of my services. Probably, who else would have cared enough?

I never went back to Thomas's place. After the funeral, we didn't see him again. He packed up my things and laid them on our porch a few nights later. I guess having me around would remind him too much of her. He pretty much became a hermit and stayed a bachelor for the rest of his days. Of course, I knew the reason was that no one could ever take my mother's place.

Her death took a terrible toll on Granny, and I'm sure my behavior added to her grief. I refused to step inside the church again no matter how many tears she shed or how much she pleaded. I was filled with such anger and disillusionment, I withdrew from the world. I no longer had friends because I no longer wanted anyone to get close to me. No matter where I turned, nothing could ease my grief, and when Granny died, four years later, I took her death upon my shoulders, knowing I could have comforted her, but I remained stubbornly locked inside myself.

Papa and I were like two ghosts inhabiting the same house. He was a broken man after Granny died, and I had been broken since I was ten years old and sat beside my mother's body through the frozen night. Like my mother, I graduated from high school at sixteen, and because I had nothing better to do, I enrolled at the state university.

Papa died the first semester I was away at college. I think he only held on until his job of raising me was finished, and he felt free to join the woman who made him whole. As the only survivor, I inherited all their worldly goods, which spared me the anguish of trying to hold down a job. It also left me with little ambition and no reason to have to think beyond my own demons. Surprisingly, I did well with my studies, but college is where I was introduced to liquor. Not surprising, I grabbed hold of it like a lifeline to a drowning man.

"Ha, every time I come up with an analogy, it has to do with drowning. Do you hear me? Why don't you answer me, I know you're here I can feel your presence! Come on, now, let me see you... please someone talk to me."

Orion stood silently beside his charge knowing Jack was filled with bitterness but sensing he was on the verge of a breakthrough gave him hope for this earthling that God loved. Barael was immediately by his side. Looking at the powerful angel, who he trusted without measure, Orion said, "I cannot help but feel for this one. He had a hard life, and some things were beyond his control. He seems to be drawing closer to the answers he seeks." Barael responded, "I hope you're right, Orion, but we must remember they have to come back to the Master by their own volition." Nodding in agreement, the two warriors continued the vigils they had been assigned, steadfast and unmovable as they waited for "it" to begin.

13

She was walking in front of me the first time I saw her. It was the sight of her red hair and the way she tossed her head that caused me to lose my breath. Running to get in front of her, I came face to face with the most beautiful girl I had ever seen.

I froze. My mouth hung open, and I couldn't get any words to come out. Normally, after I'd had a few drinks to start off my day, I was a wise cracking clown who kept everyone amused. I was accepted by most everyone on campus. I was quite the popular man. But in her presence, all I could do was stumble over my own feet and look like a fool.

She stood silently looking at me like she would a dimwitted dog that stopped in her path. She must have been somewhat curious for she could have simply walked around me, but she stood waiting to see if I was capable of common speech.

It wasn't much of a speech; I finally got out a croaky, "Hey."

"Hey, yourself, Can I help you?"

My courage was flowing again, and I flippantly told her, "No thanks, but you look lonely and I'm here to keep you company." It was a line I'd used many times before, and it always brought on giggles and a sure conquest for me. Sometimes, I had to work a little harder to get myself into their beds, but most of the time, it was the first date. More often than not, I'd climb out their dorm windows the next morning before the house mother could discover me. It was a time of free love, which equated to "free sex" for us males. No strings, no commitment.

I wasn't prepared for the look of sadness on her lovely face. She shook her head and said, "I was hoping for more from you. Don't waste my time again." And then she walked around me and left me standing there looking like the fool that I was. I skipped classes for the rest of the day and fought the anger at her for making me feel stupid and anger at myself for being so stupid. I lost that battle, too.

For a week, I searched for her. Everywhere I went, my eyes were constantly looking for the sight of her. No one seemed to know who she was, and I had almost given up hope of ever finding her when I stumbled into her again, and I mean literally stumbled into her. Too many drinks were becoming the norm, and my self-control was gone. I almost knocked her off her feet in front of a local hangout for students.

This time, she looked like an evil ogre had accosted her, and shrinking back from my heavy breath, she said, "You better get a grip, Jack," and stepped into the street to get around me. A few of the girls with her started laughing, and that's the part that really hurt. Could I possibly appear any dumber in her eyes?

I was appalled and embarrassed at how ridiculous I must have appeared to her. And I was dangerously close to bawling my head off right there in front of the curious bystanders that were still staring at me. Holding on to what little dignity I had left, I crept away with my tail between my legs. It was the next morning when my head cleared that I realized she knew my name. She knew my name! Holy cow, she liked me.

I spent the next week cleaning up my act, talking to professors, and trying to act somewhat respectable. I even cleaned up my room and spent three hours in the laundromat washing clothes I hadn't set eyes on for months. And all the while, a plan was forming to win that gorgeous redhead. It was the first time that I wanted something bad enough to work for it.

I only drank a few drinks each day to loosen my tongue and relax me a little. The rest of the time, I was studying and trying to get my grades up while looking for her all over campus. I had begun to think she had dropped out or was deliberately avoiding me, a distinct possibility. I was so far behind in several of my classes, that nothing but hours in the library could even get me halfway caught up. So on that late February snowy night, I found myself sitting in a quiet corner with a pile of books in front of me and desperately trying to absorb knowledge that held no interest for me.

"Well, Jack Simmons, the last person in the world I would have expected to run into in the library."

Jerking my head up, I stared into those amazing sea-green eyes and thought to myself, *How strange that the whole world comes to a standstill when she speaks.*

"Hey," was the best I could muster.

She sat down across from me and laid a pile of books between us. Opening up the top one, she proceeded to pretend to be studying intently.

I couldn't take my eyes off her. I could feel myself falling head over heels more in love with her and was terrified that if I opened my mouth, the spell would be broken, and she would disappear into thin air.

Without looking up, she said, "Jack, staring at me won't get your studying done any sooner."

I shook myself out of my stupor and said succinctly, "Uh, yeah."

We spent the next hour acting like we were studying, sitting silently across from each other. There was so much electricity in the air my hair was standing on end. The weird time finally ended; without much conversation, and she allowed me to walk her to her dorm. I stood on the front porch with the bright overhead light shining on us and faces peering at us through the windows.

"Good night, Jack. Thanks for walking me home," she said in a matter-of-fact voice, like this was no big deal and she wasn't feeling like I was. But she didn't move toward the door, just remained staring up at me with those gorgeous eyes, her lips parted ever so slightly. I couldn't help myself. I leaned in closer and lowering my head, closed my eyes and aimed for that luscious mouth.

Before I could make contact, she rudely laid both hands on my chest and gave me a shove backward. "Not on our first date, Jack," she said firmly. And then she was inside, and the door was shut in my stunned face. I stood there for several minutes trying to figure out what was really going on and then it hit me. She had said, "Not on our first date," which meant there would be others! I went from dejected to euphoric in a split second.

Grinning like a Cheshire cat, I bounded down the steps and hurried to my dorm, hoping my roommate was still out so I could lay in my bed and think about her the rest of the night.

It was the beginning of a life change for me. I saw her every moment she would allow me to. And when I wasn't with her, she consumed my thoughts. The only flaw about her was her deep commitment to her religion. She never said the word "religion", but she would bring up Jesus name at the most inopportune times, and it made me feel awkward whenever she did that. I was too afraid of losing her to tell her to lay off talking about God. I had spent years driving Him out of my life. He had deserted me when I needed Him, and I wouldn't make the mistake of trusting Him again.

It took me weeks to get to first base with her, and the more she turned me down, the more my desire for her grew. We were getting into heavy petting with every date and still she would stop me when things were going like I wanted. I had never had so much trouble getting a girl to go "all the way" when I set my mind to it. We had been steady dating for a couple of months when I finally got so frustrated I yelled at her, "What is wrong with you? Either you love me or you don't. If this is the way it's going to be, then we need to end this now!"

We were in the front seat of my latest car. For some ridiculous reason, she refused to climb into the back seat with me. I was so filled with anger at this last turn down it took me a minute to realize she was crying. Her sobs were getting louder, and it tore at my heart to have hurt her.

"Honey, I'm sorry. You know I didn't mean it. It's just that I love you, and I want to show you how much I love you."

"Jack, I love you, too, but I've told you over and over I can't do this unless we are married."

"All right, all right! Then let's get married."

"Do you mean it, or are you just saying it?" She was looking at me with those fabulous eyes still glistening with her tears.

"I mean it. But let me do this right. Sue Ann Richner, will you do me the tremendous favor of marrying me and putting me out of this misery? Oh, and will you consent to growing old with me?"

It wasn't much of a proposal, but it was enough for her. She threw herself into my arms and kept saying over and over, "Yes, Jack. Yes, yes, yes!" And then she allowed me to talk her into the back seat, and she lost her virginity the night I said all the right things.

I wasn't expecting her to cry when we were finished. I thought maybe I had hurt her, but I was trying to be gentle knowing it was her first time. "Jack, I'm not hurt, but we should have waited until we were married."

"Now, honey, we're as good as married. Don't cry anymore." And I held her in my arms, feeling pleased and satisfied with her and with myself.

I was on top of the world. Everything had fallen into place, and it was great for two whole months. Just four weeks before I was to graduate, she hit me with news that shook me out of my state of self-satisfaction.

We were standing on the sidewalk in front of the library where she had asked me to meet her. Looking up at me with this terrified expression, she said, "Jack, I'm late."

"Late for what?" I asked her not understanding what she meant.

"I think I may be pregnant, and I'm scared!" Her bottom lip was trembling, and her eyes were pooling up tears.

I thought I'd been hit with a rocket. "Are you sure?"

"No, but I'm never late, and now I'm past due by almost two weeks!"

She looked like she might go into hysterics, so I put my arms around her and pulled her tightly against my chest hoping the shaking was coming from her and not me.

Trying to slow down my heart so it wouldn't explode, I said, "Don't worry, sweetheart, it's probably just nerves. But if you are, then we'll up the wedding date and get married as soon as I graduate. Sue Ann, I love you, so let me do the worrying from now on. Okay?"

100

And I did plenty of it over the next few weeks. With term papers due, consoling Sue Ann, and trying to figure out how I was going to support a family, I went back to more than my customary two drinks a day. I was good at keeping it hidden since I had developed a taste for vodka. Sue Ann had no idea I was drinking let alone how much.

I don't know when, or how, she broke the news to her folks. But they weren't in attendance when we graduated. We packed up our few belongings and drove to Sue Ann's hometown. It was awkward when she introduced me to her mother and father, but I imagine it was just as awkward for them. I checked into a local hotel and waited for the details to be worked out. It didn't take long. Time was running out or the bride would be wearing a maternity frock. I knew the ceremony was not going to be what Sue Ann had dreamed of, but she didn't complain.

Our wedding was a small affair with no one from my side of the family in attendance, and her mother and father sitting tight-lipped on the front row. A few close friends and relatives sparsely seated on one side of the church. We were married by the elderly preacher who had married her folks and baptized Sue Ann. Maybe it was my imagination, but he seemed to be tight-lipped whenever his gaze set on me. The reception was a quiet venue without the benefit of alcoholic beverages. They didn't even condone wine, which I thought was strange. The stories I remembered about Jesus was Him turning water into wine. It was the miracle that impressed me most as an adult.

Things were happening fast. I was now a married man. I had a whole new family that I was trying to win over, and I would soon be a father. If I hadn't loved her so much, I'd have run as far as I could away from this situation, but I did love her, and the thought of living without her was unthinkable.

14

The whole town seemed to have circled our nuptials on their calendars. Maybe I was being skeptical, but the older women seemed to be rallying around my mother-in-law as if she was the one needing support. Baby Robert was born six months after the wedding. He was a perfect, happy, baby and won over everyone including the preacher. Even my harshest critics did an about face after spending time with Robert. I guess I couldn't be all bad if I had fathered this beautiful child.

I bought into a car dealership with the last of my inheritance and found my niche in life. I could talk anyone into anything if I had enough to drink beforehand. Sue Ann got her figure back in record time and also became pregnant again in record time. I wasn't too pleased with the situation but deciding it was probably my fault I had a private conversation with my doctor and decided to get myself fixed on the QT. We had become drinking buddies on the sly, so he was willing to perform the minor surgery on a Saturday morning before he met his golfing buddies at the country club.

It was fast and not too painful, and I told Sue Ann I was coming down with the flu or something and needed a couple of days in bed alone. I kept a flask hidden in my side of the closet. It lasted me the few days I hid out and rested. She was the perfect wife, worrying over my health, waiting on me hand and foot, and she was still taking care of Robert while carrying our second child in her large belly. She was too far along for us to be having any fun in bed so she never suspected a thing. By the time baby Charlotte came along, I was healed nicely and couldn't wait to have my beautiful wife back under me.

With two children, our small two-bedroom house was crowded to the rafters. I didn't like stepping over toys and edging around high chairs so I decided we needed a bigger place, and besides, the dealership was making money, and we should be moving up. I deserved better than what we had.

Sue Ann, ever the voice of reason, said, "But, Jack, we're just now starting to save some money. Why don't we wait another year? Who are we trying to impress?"

When she talked like that, I could feel my temper start to flare. I was the one who was working and bringing home the money to her. She needed to respect me and not disagree with every idea I had. I wanted to yell at her and tell her I was the head of this household, and I wasn't going to put up with this much longer. Instead of yelling the words at her, I stomped out and spent several hours at a shabby bar on the outskirts of town. No one in our social circle was apt to run into me there. It wasn't the kind of place they frequented. I stayed until I figured Sue Ann had learned her lesson, a tactic that had worked before, and it worked again this time.

When I staggered in after midnight, and more than a little tipsy, she was so scared that I might not be coming back at all, she gave in and we spent the next couple of weeks hunting for a house more to my liking.

It was a somewhat grand two-story white traditional with a white picket fence that fit in well on the treelined street. I was filled with pride at what I had been able to provide for my family, but I knew that secretly Sue Ann was worried over the large mortgage. She mentioned once that if we were to have more children, it would be difficult to manage all the expenses. I came close to revealing my little secret to her then, but at the last minute, I decided not to try explaining why I had kept it from her. What she didn't know couldn't hurt her.

We were mostly happy. Our biggest problem was her constant begging for me to attend church with her and the kids. By Saturday,

I would start to tighten up knowing what was coming. And sure enough, it never seemed to fail. Then this one Saturday, she must have been really desperate, she coyly approached me with, "Jack, I've been thinking about the business, and I think I have an idea on how to increase sales."

That got my attention. Sue Ann knew nothing about business. But I said, "Okay, babe, what's your idea?"

"Well, there are a lot of business people that attend our church. I know that once they spend some time with you, they will be so impressed. You could speak with them after services, and I'm sure that would open up a whole new clientele."

When she came up with that one, I was overcome with laughter. I picked her up and swung her around the living room while she pretended to be offended. "Sweetheart, don't try to con a pro. I invented that one." I couldn't stop laughing at her feeble attempt to trick me.

"Jack, you're a good father and a good man, but don't you see that your example will have a negative effect on Robert and Charlotte as they get older?"

She just couldn't leave well enough alone. My mood quickly swung from laughter to anger, and I stormed out of the house ignoring her pleas to come back and talk this out. I headed for the office where I kept a good stash of liquor and after a couple of stiff ones I settled down and drove back to finish our little talk.

She was in the kitchen doing her eternal cleaning when I walked into the room. "Sue Ann, I'm going to tell you this just once, and then I don't want you to bring up this subject again!" She turned toward me and I could see her eyes were red and swollen from crying over this current episode. Instead of being moved by her tears, I felt the anger well up again, but I pushed it down and tried to speak in a reasonable voice, like I would to a child.

"I believe that the kids should get to choose whether they want to believe like you do or like I do. So let's not argue about this again. Now come here and let me show you what I think of you, my lovely wife." It worked... for a while.

She and the kids were faithful members of the First Baptist Church, attending most of the services and volunteering at every opportunity. She stopped hounding me to go with them, and I felt that I had finally won. The main dissent in our otherwise happy marriage had been removed. I was content.

At my insistence, we joined the Country Club, and I belonged to the most important civic organizations. I was a well-known man about town and was considered a successful businessman, even without ever setting foot inside the First Baptist Church. Sue Ann kept busy with things she volunteered for at the church and a few local charities. She was still looking good, and I felt good about my life even without the excitement we had in the beginning.

But day by day, I needed more liquor to get me through. It happened so slowly I didn't see it coming. The years passed so fast I lost some of them, and I was losing my youth. I was starting to feel like an old man. Robert was graduating from high school, and Charlotte would be a senior next year. It was all slipping away, and I didn't know how to make it slow down.

Then we hired a new gal at the dealership. She was tall and willowy, and every male in the place was panting over her, me included. Talking to her made me feel like a big man again, not just a middle aged, over the hill, has been.

I couldn't wait to get to work now. And when I was away from the office, I thought of a thousand reasons to call in just to hear her voice. She was flirty and fun, and she made me feel like a teenager again. I was back on top of my game.

Even Sue Ann noticed the difference. "You seem particularly jovial, Jack, something good happening at work?" she asked me with a seemingly innocent expression. But I knew my face flushed, and I attacked her before she could ask me anymore questions.

"What do you mean by that? What's the matter with you, Sue Ann? Sometimes, it seems like you deliberately set out to try to make me mad! You can ask the stupidest questions, woman!" I stormed out of the house before she had time to answer, but I had a feeling she could read my mind, and if that was so, I was in a mass of trouble.

The gorgeous Reba was alone in the office when I got there. I rushed past her, stomped into my office, and slammed the door. I jerked the bottle of vodka from the bottom drawer and poured myself a good half glass. I was just about to take a long swig when there was a timid knock on the door. She opened it without waiting for me to give her an invitation, and stepped inside, closing the door behind her.

"I'm sorry to bother you, Jack, but is something wrong?" She came up to my desk and stood there looking beautiful and anxious. "Is there anything I can do to help?"

I could think of several things, but I had a quick conversation with myself and told self, *Whoa, slow down, boy. Don't scare her off.* So instead of saying something, I shook my head and tried to look sorrowful at the same time.

"Well, its past quitting time so do you mind if I join you in a drink?" Reba was looking at me like a cat with a mouse, and I knew she was way ahead of me. We had several drinks together until everyone else had gone and the place was locked up.

We both knew what was going to happen, and that voice that was forever at me was getting louder inside my head. I shut it up with another drink and then Reba was in my arms, and it was like being back in college before Sue Ann came into my life and turned me into an old man.

It was only the beginning. I couldn't get enough of her. I started making excuses to be away from home several nights a week, and I was drinking heavier than I ever had before. We stopped being cautious during the days at the dealership. She spent more time in my office with the door locked than she did at her desk. She consumed me, and it wasn't long before everyone at work was aware of the affair. So, of course, it became grist for the gossip mill all over town. I guess Sue Ann was told by well-meaning friends who couldn't keep it to themselves, the bunch of busy bodies!

Six months after the affair began, I was stunned when Sue Ann walked into the office on a Friday afternoon just before closing. I wasn't happy to see her. She rarely came to the dealership, and I never made it a point of welcoming her into my territory. She usually stayed where she belonged. Looking at her face, I had the sinking feeling… she knows.

I was going to try to start this off with me getting the upper hand, but before I could say a word, she firmly took over.

"I have something to tell you, Jack. It won't take long so you just sit there and listen." She was standing over me, and I had never seen her so furious. Up until now, she had always had such resilience, going along with me no matter what. I knew before she said another word, she was through backing up.

"Your clothes are in the parking lot out front. I have filed for divorce. I will keep the house. You will pay for the children's education until they get out of college. You will pay me alimony for the next five years. My attorney will be contacting you tomorrow, but I wanted to deliver this news myself." She swallowed deeply, the anger faded, and a look of profound sadness came across her face. The last words she said to me were, "No one will ever love you like I did, Jack. You were my life, my heart. Now, I can't bear the sight of you!"

She was never more beautiful than she was at that moment, and it hit me like a ton of bricks that my life was over, and I was powerless to get it back. The voice was loudly telling me, "I tried to tell you, Jack, what a fool you are. You won't win her back this time. This time, it's over." The voice was right.

I got myself a lawyer who, living in the same town, was well aware of my infidelity and advised me to accept whatever terms were offered me. I did. Sitting across the table from Sue Ann, I started to plead with her, but both lawyers quickly put a stop to my sniveling and within minutes, it was over. She never looked back as they walked out of the room. I was a free man. Free to do whatever I wanted, but I wanted to go home and start over, and I had lost all desire for the sexy Reba. She was starting to get on my nerves, and within a couple of weeks, I laid her off and hired a woman three times her age who could work faster and didn't distract the hired help.

It wasn't long before business was down. I was hitting the bottle constantly, and people started avoiding me wherever I went. Robert's graduation was a disaster. I just wanted to talk to him, but I was too drunk to stand up, and the evening ended when several guys dragged me away and took me home to my apartment.

It was a short downhill slide after that; of course, I was already well on my way to the bottom. The business went bankrupt and was soon under new management. I hit rock bottom then, or thought I had, but there was more to come.

Two years after the divorce, Sue Ann wed her divorce attorney, and half the town showed up for their nuptials. Up until that moment, I held out hope that somehow I could win her back. I gave up then and spiraled even deeper into the bottle, no family, no friends, no life. My children were ashamed to be seen with me, so there was no one for me to complain to about how my life had turned out.

During the darkest times, I started thinking about Granny and how safe I had felt then. There was nowhere to feel safe anymore. So I climbed into my constant companion and pulled the cap down and tried to drown my sorrows. It was four years after the divorce and right after my forty-fifth birthday (which nobody remembered) that I took the plunge into the icy water and ended up here.

Now what? Am I supposed to continually relive my sad tale over and over? I can't stand this, but I can't make it stop.

***

Orion stood at a distance, his features locked in anger as he watched the demons surrounding his charge, the demons of remorse, pride, doubt, shame, and guilt, all attacking at the same time, tormenting Jack relentlessly, knowing he could wipe them out in a moment if given a sign from Michael. How much longer would he be commanded to stand idly by and allow these obscene creatures of Lucifer to have their way? Unconsciously, his hand dropped to the hilt of his sword.

He took one step forward and ran directly into Aaron. "Don't lose control now, Orion. I know how difficult it is to watch their suffering over the decades, but this is our task. Michael has told me that the time is almost at hand when all will be revealed to us. Stand firm and wait."

Aaron's words hit Orion like a thunderous lightning bolt. He knew the truth of the words that had been spoken. He also knew how close he had come to disobeying Michael and that was something he had never done over the eons of time. Quickly, Barael joined them, and the three warriors steadied themselves with the knowledge that this time will pass and then the King of kings will take His eternal revenge on Lucifer and his legions.

But for now, it is a time of waiting... for now.

PART 4

2061

"The final four together."

15

"Well, good morning, Miss Lydia. And how are you feeling today, dearie?"

"I try not to think on it overly. I might discover I'm not doing too good and that would upset me."

I was watching her through narrowed eyes, and truthfully, her reaction didn't surprise me. She froze in place, her hand still holding the rod that opened the blind on my one window. She must have asked this same question a hundred times over the past seven years and not once had she heard me utter a single word, let alone a response to anything she said.

She slowly turned around and I quickly shut my eyes but not before seeing the unhealthy pallor her face had become. Her voice was shaky as she stood rigid in front of the window. "What did you say, Miss Lydia... Miss Lydia?"

Oh, how awful of me to tease her like this, but I just couldn't help myself. Now, I mustn't laugh out loud or she will know I have come alive again and then all hell will break loose. "Excuse me, Lord, I didn't mean to swear, but I'm not real sure that hell is a curse word. Is it? If it is, then forgive me, and if it isn't, then save that forgiveness for the next time."

Things began to change about ten days ago when I came out of a long darkness and became myself again. I know who I am, where I am, and how long I've been here. My brain seems to be in overdrive, but this ole worn-out body is still useless. Irritating as that is, I am amazed that all the things that were fuzzy have become sharply clear. I seem to have better vision than when I was a young woman, but the clarity of my eyes is only a small part of the new me. The people who come into contact with me, people who never speak as they go about trying to feed me and keep me somewhat clean, are being revealed in an astonishing way. I can see, like in a vision, what their lives are like, what sadness and grief they are suffering or what is making them happy as they go about living their lives.

I have to say I am thoroughly enjoying this new insight, but I have a feeling that God has a different reason for this gift other than to just keep me amused. Hmm, He has never been one to move hastily, and I have learned to have a certain patience when dealing with Him.

It feels so good to be alive again. I know I haven't died yet, but the blackness, the lack of any stimulation was worse than death. Now I can reflect on my many years on this earth, force myself to inhale slowly until my lungs are full and relish the sensation. I don't know how long this gift will remain, but I will cherish this time for as long as He will let me.

It must have been over eight years ago when fatigue began to overcome me on a daily basis. A slow erosion of my mind and body began as the light gradually faded until there was nothing but a frightening darkness and I lost myself. By then, my beautiful children had died ahead of me. That's one of the painful results of living so long. The first child to go was my baby girl, Opal. I thought I might actually die from the grief that settled over me during those days. Clyde, my husband of over fifty years, had passed away a decade before, so there was no one to share the debilitating anguish that comes with losing a child. And then one by one, the other three were gone, and their children gathered around me to comfort me as best they could.

Thirteen beautiful grandchildren grew up to become adults with different viewpoints and beliefs. Some would follow in my footsteps as grateful children of God, others would shut their eyes and ears to anything to do with my loving Father and, it seems, all my fervent prayers did not change the fact that they had free will and chose not to believe.

Things have changed so drastically over my lifetime. In my youth, people were still able to worship freely and openly. The loss of organized religion began gradually and gained momentum as the years unfolded. Condemnation of Christians came from all fronts until most places of worship had simply been abandoned or sold for other purposes. Religious practices were zealously accused of being intolerant, and if you openly declared your love for the Heavenly Father, you were, at the least, laughed at and ostracized from society.

For us older Christians, we balanced precariously between what used to be and what was coming. To prepare our children to live and thrive in the world was difficult and for the next generation almost impossible. I watched my grown children as they valiantly tried to instill a faith into their own by homeschooling them with the outdated books of learning, which were abandoned as obsolete by the school systems. My grandchildren learned world history, civics, great literature, none of which was taught in the mass public school systems.

I hate this horrible malaise that pulls me down when I let myself dwell on the things of today. The changes are without precedent for never in all of history has the world become so small and conflicting. Some things developed into great benefits for all of us. Medical advances were a godsend. Cancer, Parkinson's, diabetes, all eradicated in less than a decade once they found the common denominator. Oh, there are many marvelous inventions including the microchips implanted under the skin of our right hands, enabling us with a single swipe the ability to purchase whatever we choose without the hassle of carrying the old plastic credit cards. Cash stopped being accepted soon after Opal passed away. Mail delivery was abandoned shortly after that as everyone had computers built into complex home offices.

I am beginning to wonder if the "darkness" overtook me or if I willingly allowed it just to escape this world. I think the final straw came when the beautiful old cathedral in New York City, with its awesome stained glass windows, was razed. The massive church took over a century to build and was destroyed in a day. Crowds cheered as it was brought down to be replaced with more high-rise buildings to house the growing number of the population that is out pacing our resources.

I believe seeing that centuries old church being demolished grieved me to the core. Occasionally, an episode of a home burning due to what the media reporters said was another hateful crime directed against religious fanatics was reported; a crime that seldom was solved or investigated. No wonder so many of the faithful have not been able to withstand the onslaught of prejudice and violence directed at them.

It grieves my heart over my lost ones; this grief is even heavier than losing my children to death because I am aware that I will see them again. Oh, for heaven's sake, here I've been given this amazing gift of clarity, and I go wasting time stewing over things I can't control. "Lord, you just lead me and let me know what I'm supposed to do with this. And in the meantime, I shall continue to pretend to be blind and out of it, for I have a strong hunch that is your wish."

There's a certain excitement today, I can feel it. Possibly because I know it is all about me. Today is my birthday, my 102nd birthday. One hundred and two years old! I never in all my life thought I would live this long. If I'm truthful, I have to admit there were several times when I would gladly have stopped breathing. Times of such grief, when living was harder than dying, times when pain overcame everything.

But reliving it all again, as I have been doing since God gave me a lucid mind, I'm coming to the realization that all in all, I'm fairly pleased with my life. The devastating times were when I drew closer to Him and when those times had passed, I was all the stronger for them. If given the chance, I wouldn't change things, not even the horrible times, because without them, how would I have known how precious time with loved ones can be?

I'm listening to the aides around me, clucking and chattering about the cake and all the people who are coming. These sweet girls are spending way too much time trying to decide what dress they should put on me, like I am their own personal baby doll. They don't have many choices and what there are must be totally out of date. It's been over a decade since any new clothes were bought for me. I'll admit, I was somewhat of a clothes horse in my day. I loved getting gussied up and going out with close friends. Those friends have been gone for a long time now.

These two aides are kind and that can't be said for some who work here. I am amazed that anyone would do what they have to do every day and still remain gentle spirits. I've not been abused, no, just mostly ignored. In fairness, it would be exceedingly difficult to become attached to a living vegetable. A conversation has to be a two-way street, and my inability to communicate has kept me a voiceless, witless stranger to them.

The noise is growing louder outside my door. Taking a deep breath, I'm starting to have second thoughts. Am I really sure that I want to meet strangers who have come here out of curiosity to see what a really old woman looks like? I'm almost ready to put a stop to this. I don't even know most of those people. All I have to do is open my mouth and tell these girls to forget it and let them inform the guest that the party has been cancelled! It sounds like a mass of humanity is waiting for my appearance, and these two are in a heated argument over which outdated ensemble looks best with my hair. They are determined to have me at my best when I am wheeled out before the waiting crowd to be ogled at like a strange animal in a zoo.

"Father, what do you want me to do? Why have you given me this gift? Surely, it is for more than this moment?" My racing heart is slowing down, and somehow, I know I am to face this. "All right, Lord, I will do as you say, but no one had better make fun of this aging woman, or I will give them a what for!"

Finally, we're ready. Silence settles over the huge room as the two loyal aides wheel me out of the segregated Alzheimer's unit into the reception area reserved for the likes of this. My stars, the room is overflowing with people, and I have to be careful to not let them know I can actually see and hear. I let my head droop down to hide my eagerness as one by one they come by and awkwardly acknowledge their relationship to me and wish me... what, best wishes and a hope for many more years? I do feel sorry for them. If they were honest, they would wish me a speedy death. But I must have instilled some manners into my own, who passed those good manners on to their children, and that pleases me more than it should. Pride is not a good thing, but I cannot help but think on the fact that without me, none of these people would be alive. Ha, maybe a little pride won't totally ruin an old woman.

The line never seems to end as they keep coming to my side and telling me who they are. My visions are coming so fast I can't keep up with them. My head is beginning to ache from the sheer effort of trying to concentrate. I didn't realize I would grow this tired so quickly. The vivid visions of each of them has taken a huge amount of concentration and drained me emotionally. It breaks my heart to see what each of them has endured and so many have lost their faith. I am deeply grateful for my age. I would not want to be a minute younger and have to face what these loved ones will be subject to. I cannot imagine what will happen to them in the future.

I can't seem to concentrate on who is who anymore. A heavy exhaustion is covering me, and I can't hear what they are saying. Oh dear, I can feel the darkness beginning again.

I cannot get a good breath.

"Wait, Lord, just a few more minutes, please…"

16

Those were to be the last thoughts Lydia Young was to have on this earth, at least as a living being.

Opening her eyes, she saw absolutely nothing, only darkness, no light to expose where she was, but she was receiving conscious thought. Slowly, she began to realize she was enclosed in some kind of whirling vortex. The spinning never stopped, and she was acutely aware of being cocooned inside the constantly moving darkness. It wasn't uncomfortable, she wasn't dizzy, and there was no desire for food or drink. But Lydia was completely and totally aware she was no longer among the living, and she had no idea how long she had been in this weightless, silent, spinning chamber.

Vaguely, she felt something else was with her inside the spinning mass, a kind of mist or fog, a moistness that surrounded her. She felt a strange peace and calmness throughout her body. She was getting used to not having to think or make decisions and was content to be lost in this safe haven.

Suddenly, a blinding light split the whirling chamber into shards, and a powerful surge of energy dropped her sharply downward and she found herself reeling upright on her feet in a place she had never been before. Blinking rapidly, her eyes gradually came into focus. Steadying herself at this sudden change from whirling darkness to standing upright in the sunlit stillness, she looked around at her surroundings and realized she was standing in the middle of a very old cemetery. Then a bevy of questions and thoughts threatened to engulf her.

"Where am I? Is this somewhere on earth? What a lonely neglected place."

To her amazement, she was no longer the crippled centenarian. Her youth had been restored; her newly rejuvenated body was now in its prime. It was a glorious feeling to have control of both her body and her mind.

"Thank you, Lord," was Lydia's immediate response.

The sun was shining, and Lydia stared up at it as if she had never seen the center of her universe before. There was no need for her to shield her eyes from its harmful rays. Normal things no longer seemed to have an effect on her. Trying to think rationally, she surmised from its position to be around noon, but she felt no warmth from its rays. For a time, she was too confused to move, but not seeing or hearing another person, she began to hesitantly, cautiously, explore her surroundings.

The cemetery was centuries old, according to the faded inscriptions on the crumbling tombstones scattered throughout the grounds. There were long neat rows in some areas, but in others, the monuments were placed helter-skelter as though bodies had been buried where they fell. As she threaded her way slowly throughout the grounds, peering at the names engraved upon the headstones, she felt no awareness that she had ever known any of those laid to rest here.

At a loss as to why or how she came to be here, she almost wished she were back in the comforting confines of the whirling darkness. Aware that time was passing, she continued to explore the unfamiliar grounds and discovered a small one room church in a far corner near the old dirt road running alongside the west entrance to the grounds. The crumbling stones that once had been proud walls were testimony that this church, like so many others, had obviously been abandoned years ago.

A feeling of profound sadness engulfed her as she stood inside the high-pitched room with the broken windows that lined both sides of the small church. The roof was mostly gone with only the oak rafters still in place. It stood as a testament to the carpenter who created this small building. She had the feeling this chapel, built to honor a loving God, was hanging on for dear life, refusing to let the generations defeat it. Feeling a need to cry, she was surprised there were no tears, and yet, she knew she was weeping. Something about being in a place of worship, even one as decrepit as this one, made her soul ache.

Why she should feel such a profound loss simply by standing alone in this dilapidated old building was beyond her understanding. She quickly stepped outside and once again lifted her eyes to the sun.

"Why am I here?" she whispered softly, afraid to speak in her natural voice as any noise might awaken something frightening within these grounds. The question was echoing inside her head until she thought she would burst from the pressure, and then Lydia Young did the unthinkable, she screamed with all her might, "GOD, WHY AM I HERE?"

After her loud outburst, she felt much better, more at peace, and even a little contrite for raising her voice to Almighty God. But it did seem to have cleared her head of so much confusion. Taking in a deep breath of the warm mid-day air, she continued her search through the grounds, as memories washed over her—memories so vivid it was as if she were living them for the first time.

She remembered being very young and living at home with Momma and Daddy. Without conscious thought, she was transported back into the unforgettable family setting—the sounds, the smells—of the home she grew up in and the family that made up her universe. Like old photographs, they drew her into a time that had ceased long ago.

Since she was totally alone, she found the sound of her own voice comforting, as she spoke out loud as events unfolded.

"Momma was large boned, with a constant smile on her full face. Being held on her ample lap was the safest place in the world to be."

Lydia felt the warmth of those arms as she closed her eyes and reclaimed the times of her childhood. "I must have been around three or four on that day," she said, nodding her head in agreement to her words. The scene played out in her mind, so clear the images were strikingly powerful as she saw herself lifting her little hands to both sides of Momma's face, as her shrill young voice resonated through the years, "No, Momma, no. You sing now!"

Momma's laughter filled the room, and Lydia giggled in response, knowing that she had talked Momma into postponing the next chore on her list and now she had Momma's undivided attention. Settling deeper into the comforting lap, she waited for the cherished voice to begin. Momma leaned back in the kitchen chair and began to sing. It didn't take long for the soothing voice to lull Lydia into sleep, and unable to rouse herself, did not raise a fuss as she felt the warmth of Momma's arms carrying her securely to the room she shared with her big sister. Without protest, she stretched out on the small bed as the faded comforter was placed gently over her.

"Strange that the most vivid scenes I have of Momma are always tied to the lilting beauty of her voice lifted in song. She sang a multitude of hymns, from memory, with a sweet voice, surprising for her large girth. We seldom saw her motionless, it seemed her hands were constantly busy doing chores that she never seemed to tire of.

"Daddy was a man of small stature, who loved his wife and children with happy abandonment. He was mostly bald, but Momma said when she met him, his hair was thick and curly. She teased him that he had become too vain about his good looks, and God probably thought it would help his character if he had less temptation. I never heard either of them raise their voices in anger, and if something was bothering them, they must have worked things out after their children were sound asleep.

"On occasion, Daddy would stop in the middle of a chore and relate one of his favorite Bible stories from the ragged old Bible that was nearly worn out from years of study. He worked constantly to feed us and to care for his brood. His face was lined from years of hard labor, but you would never find a man more content with his lot in life. He was a thankful man who loved his family and his God with all his heart, and Momma shared the center of his heart.

"I can't remember if they ever told us how they came to find each other. We didn't have grandparents or other close relatives so it was just us." Lydia spoke her thoughts out loud and shook her head as if speaking to someone near her.

Staring up at the sky, she spoke as if she was looking into the face of God. "I thought when I died, I would be with you and all my family who had gone before me. Why have you put me here? I know there is a reason, but if you would just show me what you want from me, I will obey you. You know I will." She waited for a response, but no answer came to her.

Time passed like a clock that was set on rapid time. The seasons came and went and came back again as Lydia continued to relive the years of her life, memories so intense, she was beginning to see where every decision she ever made had profound and long-lasting consequences—consequences that affected all the days of her life, like ripples on a pond when a stone was thrown into its midst.

Contenting herself with waiting for a word from heaven, she roamed the grounds and tried not to be discouraged. Feeling a freedom that pleased her, she let herself pull the precious memories from deep inside her mind and shutting her eyes, lifted her face toward the sun and sniffed the air.

"I can smell the pines when the wind blows from the south. It carries the scent of the loblolly pines across this place. I remember loblollies. We used to have them on our land. Daddy loved the look of the tall stately trees and the fragrance of them. We gathered boughs and made wreaths during Christmas. The smell of them filled the whole house."

With the heightened suggestion from the aromatic pines, more memories arose fresh in her mind. Speaking out loud, she voiced each memory as it appeared. The sound of her own voice made it seem less lonely, and she tried not to let herself think she might spend eternity roaming throughout the abandoned cemetery.

"Daddy knew all the trees and plants on our small acreage and filled our heads with their names and always reminded us they were created by a Heavenly God. He told us stories of our ancestors, who sailed across the vast ocean to escape the oppression of their native lands, to live in freedom in this country. In those days, America opened its doors and welcomed all who needed sanctuary and a safe haven to raise their families."

Lydia roamed freely inside the grounds of the small, neglected cemetery day after day and let her mind delve deeper into memories she had long forgotten, reliving them over and over, until all had come to light and she saw her life complete. The revelations unleashed by the memories brought her peace, and with the peace came the knowledge they had been shown her for a reason. But not knowing the "why" of it brought another round of questions for which she had no answers.

Time passed unnoticed until another snowfall brought her to full consciousness of her surroundings. Realizing she had been in this place through a multitude of changing seasons, she looked up at the grey clouds blocking out the sun overhead and spoke out loud, "Father, why am I here? I have loved you and been faithful to you all my life. I know there is a purpose for this, but I don't understand what I am supposed to do now? I am filled with gratitude for this gift of seeing my life lived over again, but why am I here in this place? This is not what I envisioned heaven to be. If so, then where are the streets of gold and my palace you promised? I know you have a plan, but I'm not sure what you have in mind for me. I don't feel like Eve, and for sure, this is not the garden of Eden." She continued to walk as she communicated with Almighty God and finished her prayerful communication with, "I will wait as patiently as I can to hear your voice."

And for the first time, she felt a presence near her, as if she were not as alone as she had thought herself to be. Eagerly, she quickly turned around in a circle, expecting to see someone, anyone that she could talk to, and perhaps receive the answers she desperately needed. There was no sign of anyone, but the feeling was growing stronger that she was not alone and that more than one person or thing was close by. A shiver ran up her spine, and her eyes darted across the deserted grounds.

Shaking her head as if to dispel her fears, she said, "I wonder if my body is buried here. Could that be possible?" But she knew she had searched throughout the grounds, examining all the readable headstones, and there was no one with even the hint of her name. Actually, there were no headstones with a date later than forty years ago.

"The last I remember before the blackness came over me was that most states were requiring bodies to be cremated, with the ashes stored in storage areas, and then taken into space and released in the outer regions."

"I wish I knew where I am and why I'm here." We lived many places during our lives together, but when Clyde retired, we moved back to Oklahoma and settled in the northeast corner of the state where Arkansas and Kansas are close neighbors. I don't believe I have ever seen this place. There is a strange peace here, but occasionally, I have a vague sense of danger circling around me." Her random thoughts continued as the questions plagued her without let up.

Daily, Lydia walked across the five acres of land surrounded by the crumbling sandstone fence and peered at the grounds beyond. It seemed to be uninhabited by nearby homes, and traffic along the narrow road was virtually nonexistent. The hard red clay would not be conducive to growing any kind of crops, which probably explained the lack of people in the area.

She found herself returning again to the old church, and sitting down on one of the few remaining pews allowed herself to reflect upon the world she no longer inhabited. During her life, it had morphed into a living nightmare and became a frightening place filled with chaos. "I don't know how long I have been here, but things on earth must be near a critical stage."

"Vertical farming and rooftop gardens were becoming common-place throughout the nation when I was first placed in the 'home'. Our food chain was drastically curtailed as earth warmed to alarming degrees. The southwestern United States and parts of the Midwest had become almost uninhabitable desert, leaving New Mexico, Arizona, Colorado, and parts of Texas and Wyoming deserted. Those citizens were forced into other parts of the country, overcrowding cities and communities, stretching resources to the breaking point. And with that, violence in the streets had become commonplace as people desperately tried to protect what was theirs."

Lydia grew weary of the memories that had occurred on earth during her lifetime. They seemed to crowd into her mind no matter how she tried to stop them. The memories of the enormous swarms of insects were the worse.

"We lived in fear that we would be next," she whispered to herself, afraid if she voiced her fear out loud, they might come again. Shaking her head, she tried to dispel the dreadful images that were posted on the news day in and day out. A shiver ran through her body thinking about that horrible time. Every country dreaded the next place they would appear. Around the globe, the world's largest insect swarms emerged in different locations, mostly in Third World countries, killing humans, livestock, and everything in their paths. "Why is it that the weakest seem to always be the first to be attacked?" She shook her head in bewilderment at the question that had never been answered when she was alive, and she was no closer to an answer now.

"So many of the insecticides that were common when I grew up had been banned, forcing scientists from all countries to pool their resources and desperately search for something powerful enough to wipe them out. They were finally eradicated, but not before the death tolls were staggering."

The visions continued, and Lydia felt like she was on a train traveling hundreds of miles per hour, and outside her windows, the downfall of earth played out in a never-ending panorama.

Wind power farms began to take up large portions of the earth's surface. Without wind power, no one could survive for other outdated forms of energy had become depleted or outlawed by the environmental society. Laser driven fusion energy was just becoming a reasonable alternative for the wealthier nations.

Antarctica had become ice free during the months of April and May. Due to the melting ice caps on both poles, sea levels rose to alarming depths. Islands that had been inhabited for centuries were flooded and no longer inhabitable. Hawaii, Bangkok, Cuba, among so many others, are now submerged beneath the vast oceans. Earth has become overrun by vast numbers of refugees with nowhere to find a place to relocate. Never before in all of history have so many been alienated and lost.

Lydia hung her head and gave voice to her grief, "Lord, Lord, how much longer will you wait until you come for us? I have read your word and memorized it in my heart, and I believe your words when you promised to come back for us. If you wait many more generations, there will be no one left to gather to yourself…"

The images of the changes over her lifetime overwhelmed Lydia, but the vivid images would not stop as she tried to make some kind of sense out of it all. "So many things have happened in such a short period that Momma and Daddy would never be able to imagine what this world looks like today. Overseas, the final collapse of the European Nations sent shock waves around the world. In China, over eighty million people have died of lung diseases as pollution makes all cities in that vast country a deathly place to live. China is threatening to take over much of Europe to have a place for their struggling population."

"Warfare has become a deadly game played by leaders of all the major nations. The battlefields are now being fought over by billion-dollar military humanoid robots. War over water rights and places for the ever burgeoning world population has become so commonplace, I doubt if most of the earth's inhabitants can even imagine what a blissful place this planet once was. Poverty is rampant all over the globe, unrest, wars and rumors of war have become constant."

Lydia's shoulders slumped with the weight of sadness that covered her. "Lord, I thought when I died, there would be no more weeping, and I would find peace. But these images of what used to be, and what has now become common, break my heart. Please, Father, tell me what am I doing here?" But the relentless visions continued without letup, attacking her as if intent on driving her to the ground.

"So many decisions are now being made by quantum computers that the common man's thinking has been reduced to simply obeying orders. The leaders of the world governments are intent on relying on the massive beast, believing the genius of the computers far more dependable than man's intellect. Perhaps the genius behind this belief is the creators of them. If so, then it will not be long before they will control all of the earths regions." Lydia pondered on this for a time, but whether she was right or wrong, there was nothing she could do. She believed with all her heart that only God could rescue a dying world.

"Our earth is on point to destroy itself as it has many of the animals. Elephants and gorillas became extinct long ago. And the threat of Bioterrorism grows greater each day."

Lydia hurriedly returned to the church, as if it were her sanctuary, and sat rigid on an old wooden pew as her mind dwelt on the condition of this earth and how far mankind has gone to destroy this beautiful creation. Before death, the healing tears helped, but now she was overcome with remorse and regrets as if she alone had been responsible.

In deep sadness, she dropped to her knees on the old worn planks, and lifting her eyes upward, she prayed, "I can't bear it anymore, Lord. I don't want to spend any more time here with nothing but my memories and my sorrows. You must have more for me to do than this, some purpose or reason for my continuing. So, I beg you, let me hear your voice. Until I know what you want me to do, I will remain here on my knees for as long as it takes!"

And Lydia knelt there with head bowed confident that the God she had loved all her life would speak.

And He did.

17

Lydia stubbornly remained on her knees listening for the Heavenly Father's voice. She had no concept of how long she had knelt there, but she felt it before she saw it, a charge like a volt of electricity that surged through her body and jolted her to her feet. Her eyes flew open and then quickly shut tight against the blinding light.

"Lydia, don't be afraid. I am Hebron, a servant of Almighty God, and I am here to help you." The voice was kind and soothing, and Lydia cautiously opened her eyes to see standing before her a large figure, robed in white with an aura of light surrounding him.

Trying to speak, she finally uttered, "Pleased to meet you, Hebron." With an intrepid spirit, she peered intently at him, studying his features and his dress. Suddenly, the mighty warrior spread his massive wings, and the old church timbers shuddered from the force. Lydia's mouth dropped open from the shock of seeing this magnificent creature's glorious countenance. She could not help herself from taking a step back.

The next thing he did shocked her even more. Throwing his head back, his long hair flowing, Hebron laughed heartily. "I'm sorry, little one, but I thought that knowing I am an angel would put you at your ease." He spoke with an eloquence that belied his great size.

A shaky smile played across her face. and she boldly answered him, her voice quivering only a little, "It actually does, Hebron. Then you are here to explain why I have been sent to this place and what God has planned for me?"

"I am here for much more than that, Lydia, but for now. I will tell you what I am allowed to reveal and nothing more."

Lydia frowned at his last words, hoping to get a clear picture of what her duties were to be but willing to talk with this mighty angel as long as he would stay with her.

Hebron drew in his powerful wings and asked her, "Would you mind if we walked outside for a while? This room feels very confining to me."

As they left the old church, the sun was shining and a gentle breeze blew softly across the expanse of grounds. Lydia felt calmness settle over her. She could not remember the last time she had felt such joy… perhaps never. Her gratitude at having someone to talk to was paramount at the moment. Being dead was not that uncomfortable after all.

Looking up at Hebron, as they walked along, she felt a deep affection for him, not as one might worship, but a sense of love nevertheless. As if he had read her mind, he stopped and turning toward her said, "Lydia, I have been with you since the day you were born. You are my charge. Because of your faith, my strength has remained strong, and I have been able to protect you throughout your life."

"Oh, so you are my guardian angel." Lydia nodded her head as if this news was the most common thing. "I felt your presence at times in my life, times when I was frightened or the few times when I was greatly tempted."

"I cannot take praise for all things, the Holy Spirit is strong in you and your faith gave you courage." Forming his words carefully, Hebron continued, "I have been assigned to tell you why you are here. The Father has an assignment for you, Lydia, and I have no doubt you are capable of carrying it out. There are things I do not know, but we shall do as we are commanded and see what happens, shall we?"

"You cannot imagine how eager I am to get started, Hebron. I have prayed constantly for some direction. I have a multitude of questions, but first I need to know some things that have bothered me greatly since I've been here. Where is this place?"

"You are in the center of Oklahoma, which is centrally located in this nation."

"Aww, so I am in Oklahoma! This place seems totally unfamiliar to me. I don't think I have ever been in this part of the state before, have I?"

"No, but you were placed in Oklahoma long ago just for this purpose."

"Hmm, now that's a surprise, but I suppose there are going to be quite a few surprises coming up, possibly for both of us, do you think?"

Hebron did not respond but smiled down on his petite charge and prepared himself for the barrage of questions he knew would be forthcoming.

Lydia thought carefully of how she wanted to phrase the questions that were swirling through her head and decided to start with an easy one. "How long have I been here, or better yet, how long have I been dead?"

"Time as you have known it no longer applies to us. It has no meaning. You are in eternity. Therefore, there is no time." Hebron patiently explained.

Nodding her head, Lydia studied on his answer. Finding it to be deeper than she wished to explore for the moment, she thought of something else. "I know I have only known you for a brief time, but you seem so familiar to me, as if we have met before. Is that possible?"

"Yes, we have met several times during your life. We are allowed to take on human form or even animal form if we deem it necessary to carry out God's purpose."

Shocked by his answer, Lydia hurriedly thought back over her life, trying to determine when a stranger might have been Hebron, but she quickly gave up and decided to get back to the present.

"Is this how it is for everyone when they die? If so, then what happened to all the promises of streets of gold and pearly gates?" She was only half joking as she looked up at Hebron.

"No, it most assuredly is not what normally happens to the saints of God's kingdom. But you have been chosen for a task no other human has ever been assigned, Lydia."

His unfathomable words hung in the air between them, pressing her into silence as she tried to digest the enormous responsibility of what Hebron had shared with her. There was no doubt in her mind that God had a mighty purpose for her to fulfill.

Hebron waited for barrage of questions, but she was surprisingly quiet. They walked in silence for some time before he heard her speak again, and this time, her voice was filled with confidence and strength. "If the Master has chosen me to accomplish a mission, then He will provide me with the ability, and I am humbled by His decision. I will hold my questions for a while and let you explain what I am to do." With this, she looked up at this angel of hers and waited for instructions.

Hebron knew she was acutely aware of the seriousness of their task and began to speak the words that had never been uttered in the history of mankind, and Lydia hung on every word.

"The Book of Life is almost complete. Only four more names are to be entered before the Lord of lords comes for His bride and the Great Tribulation begins for the rest of mankind. Three of the four are here, in this cemetery, lost and alone, waiting for some kind of direction, and your assignment is to provide them that direction and guide them back to the Heavenly Father. The gift of visions was given to you while you were alive so that you would understand what it does." He was watching intently as Lydia tried to absorb the task ahead of her, but she was clearly confused.

"It's all right, Lydia. You will be directed as you begin to assume your role. Continue to pray as you have been doing, and I will be here for you. We will begin very soon."

"Hebron, don't leave me!" Lydia reached out as if to hold onto him.

"I have never been away from your side. Whether you can see me with your eyes or not, I am always near you. You simply call my name and I will appear to you, but you must not put me in Yahweh's place. He will be the one to direct you. His Holy Spirit may speak directly to you as He has before, or I will relay to you what I am directed to explain. Take heart, my Lydia, we are beginning on a journey no one has ever traveled. We are not alone here, there are others, and I will introduce you to them as I am instructed."

Lydia dropped her arm and stepped back. Hebron was gone instantly, and she could not keep herself from saying, "Don't go too far."

She no longer tried to keep up with time as it passed but spent most of her days kneeling on the old church's plank floor preparing for what was to come. She was not foolish, never had been, but the lightheartedness that was part of her nature was now absent, and she was totally focused on what the Master was entrusting to her. Somehow, she knew that it was paramount to spend this time in deep prayer as layer after layer of doubt or misgivings gave way to an intrepid spirit as she dove deeper and deeper into her faith.

Hebron was intent on protecting his charge from the malevolent demons that were frantic to get to her. His powerful wings were seldom closed as he used them to swat and scatter the cadre of demonic beings as they tried to attack her. This was not much of a battle for the great warrior, but their sulfurous fumes were sprayed about as they went tumbling into the air, and the stench was most unpleasant. Barael, Aaron, and Orion kept a close watch, but knowing he was very capable of controlling the mass around Lydia, they waited for their time to come.

Suddenly, a deep sound reverberated across the land. The four froze like statues as they heard Michael's trumpet call for Aaron. There was no hesitation as the enormous wings spread out from Aaron's powerful back causing the wind to howl and trees to sway and bend as if a tornado was tearing across the land, but Aaron was unaware of the effects his movements had upon the land. He dove straight up through the first heaven that surrounds the earth, up through the firmament, into the farthest heavens, and finally came to stand before Michael, eager to hear why he was called.

Never before had Michael summoned one of them during their time with the charges. All of the meetings were instigated by one or the other of the gallant warrior angels, but this was different. Michael stood rigid and the sight of his face attested that this was no ordinary meeting.

Aaron did not speak, but waited for Michael to commence.

"The time is almost at hand. Lucifer has been made aware that all four of you are guarding charges in one place. He has always known that you were demoted, as we intended for him to him to believe. He was so intent on destroying God's greatest creation, turning faith into doubt, creating strife and division, and stirring hate among the creation that he gave you four little thought. But now, his supreme demons have been closely watching your movements, and they have reported that not only are all four of you gathered in one place, but you are still protecting your charges. He is aware that this does not normally happen, and he will be too curious about this to not investigate further."

Aaron remained silent, watching Michael's face as the archangel paced in a huge circle, forming the details of the plan in his mind. At last, satisfied that it was complete, he gave Aaron the instructions that would ignite the entire universe before it was over and bring the prophecies of God's Holy word to life.

"All right… tell Hebron he is to set Lydia to her task. She is to begin with Elizabeth and then move on to Jeffrey and Jack. Lydia has prepared herself wisely and is now ready. Your battle with the demons will intensify as she goes about this, so now you must each protect the other as well. When Lucifer hears of this, he will not understand the meaning, but he will surmise it is of utmost importance. And he will be sending his warrior demons to deal with you. Hebron's strength is at full measure, and as each soul is dealt with, their restored faith will bring all of you to battle ready status. Go now and set things in motion. I will be watching and readying the legions of heavenly warriors for battle."

With these words, Michael dismissed Aaron, and the events that God had known were coming before the beginning, before light destroyed the darkness, before the earth was created, before man was set in motion.

Aaron dove with haste, his enormous wings guiding him through the heavens as layer by layer he arrived at his destination anxious to speak with his fellow warriors.

They were waiting, their eyes watching for his return. He landed with force and without a word drew his sword and slew the group of demons that were gathered around Hebron and Lydia. A smile broke out on Barael and Orion's faces as they knew the bounds that held them back had been removed. Hebron smiled broadly and thanked Aaron. "What are our instructions?" They each asked the same question in unison, and Aaron quickly repeated what Michael had instructed.

"I know you are ready, but do not take our enemy for granted. Remember, we are not at our full strength so we must aide each other as needed. And Michael has cautioned me strongly to remember that Lucifer has not had warrior demons after us, but now that he is aware that something important is happening here, he will not hesitate to destroy us and our charges before God's plan can be implemented. Stay alert and be ready. Hebron, show yourself to Lydia and begin her assignment."

With his words still echoing in their heads, they each stood over their individual charges with swords drawn. This time, they would kill any and all of the amorphous demons that came in contact with their humans.

PART 5

The Awakening

18

Hebron stood behind Lydia as she kneeled with head bowed inside the confines of the tiny church. She had spent most of her days here since he first appeared to her. He waited to let her finish her prayers to the Father before calling her name.

She seemed to sense his presence, her back stiffened and she quickly ended her prayer. Rising to her feet, she turned around and faced him.

"Lydia, we must talk now."

"I'm ready."

He understood the transformation in his petite charge. Her small frame concealed a deep strength of character that was surprising, and the depth of her faith was evident on her face and radiated from her clear eyes. Yes, she was ready. God had chosen wisely, as always.

"It is time for you to meet the first soul you are to aid."

Lydia nodded without speaking and followed Hebron to a far corner of the cemetery where a figure stood facing the forest of trees beyond the sandstone wall. It was the figure of a woman dressed in strange clothes. Her hair was a deep auburn, and the dress she had on was long, falling to her ankles. She remained motionless, half in and half out of the shadows. The word "wraithlike" came to Lydia's mind as she stared intently at this pitiful young woman God was expecting her to aid.

There was a loneliness about her that was unnerving, and Lydia looked up at Hebron questioningly. "Who is she and how long has she been here?"

"You forget, there is no time here. But by earth's time, she has been here over a century and a half. As to whom she is, your gift will soon answer all your questions about her. Speak to her." And with that, he was gone. Lydia was no longer afraid and took another tentative step closer to the delicate figure, as she prayed silently for divine guidance.

Lifting her head, she stood completely still and watched the delicate creature that had been here all this time, and yet, this was the first time she had actually been allowed to see her. In the back of her mind was the thought that there are two more souls trapped inside these grounds. "Please, God, let me fulfill what you have sent me here to do." And with that plea, she took one step closer.

Trying not to startle the young woman, she spoke barely above a whisper. "Hello."

The figure froze for a moment then whirled around with an expression of sheer terror on her face. There was nothing especially unusual about her except her attire, which reminded Lydia of pictures of the western days at the turn of the nineteenth century.

"Please, don't be afraid. My name is Lydia." She waited for the figure to either bolt and run or find the courage to reply. She was pleased that there was no running, but the woman was still too shocked to answer her. Knowing the figure in front of her was as skittish as a young deer, Lydia remained where she was and forced herself to keep eye contact and smiled, hoping to appear friendly and unthreatening.

Lydia tried again, speaking slowly, "I believe that you have been here for a very long time. I am here to help you, so please talk to me. You truly have nothing to fear." Silence hung between them like a huge wall. Lydia took a deep breath and tried another way.

"What is your name, child? Then realizing that she no longer was an elderly woman and how foolish the question must have sounded to this waif in front of her, she repeated the question, "What is your name?"

"Elizabeth," the faintest whisper escaped from the woman's lips.

"That's a lovely name. I am glad to finally meet you, Elizabeth."

Lydia made no move to get closer but remained standing exactly where she was when she first greeted her. Something told her to be very patient and not hurry the young woman.

Elizabeth was shaking as if it was the dead of winter with freezing temperatures, but Lydia knew that the bodies they had now were not influenced by anything from the atmosphere. No, this was abject fear that caused her reaction. The young woman has no way of knowing whether I am an adversary or a friend. So Lydia waited. Finally, Elizabeth began to speak, almost in a whisper at first and then louder as the questions poured out of her, so fast Lydia could not make out what she was saying.

"Whoa, please slow down, I can't understand you. Don't worry, I'm not going to disappear, and I will answer all your questions as best I can." She tried to reassure and soothe this woman who had been alone for what must have seemed like an eternity.

Elizabeth paused for breath and tried again to explain how extraordinary it was to actually be able to communicate with someone. "I'm sorry. It's just that I've not seen a living soul who could see me or talk to me since I arrived here. Who are you and how did you get here? Do you know why we are here?" She had moved closer with each question until she was standing directly in front of Lydia.

"I've only recently found the answers to some of those questions myself, but would you mind if we walked to the small church? It's not far and I've grown accustomed to spending time there." Lydia was surprised to hear Elizabeth say, "I spend a great deal of time there also." The two women from totally different eras walked side by side toward a decaying ancient church where both had found solace during their time in Gable Cemetery.

Elizabeth continued to stare at the woman walking beside her as if to memorize these moments in case Lydia suddenly disappeared. Trying to reassure her that they truly were going to have their talk, Lydia glanced at her several times and smiled but did not speak again until they were seated on an old wooden pew. As they faced each other, Lydia began.

"First, I will tell you how I found myself here in this place and then you will tell me about your journey." Lydia spoke of the celebration for her 102nd birthday, about awakening inside the whirling cocoon, and about finding herself standing in the middle of Gable without a clue as to where she was or why she was here. Elizabeth was definitely stunned when she mentioned her age, and Lydia could not keep from laughing at the girl's confusion.

"You can't be!" was all that Elizabeth could say, without mentioning Lydia's journey in the swirling vortex.

"Yes, I'm afraid I am quite a few years older than you. Or I think I am. How old are you?"

"I was thirty-six when I... when I...," and she stuttered with difficulty before continuing on. "When I died and woke up here. Like you, I don't know how or why I am here." Staring at Lydia, she waited for the older woman to explain what was happening to the both of them.

Lydia took a deep breath, said a quick prayer, and began to speak. "Elizabeth, you are one of three who were brought here when they died. I don't have all the answers you are seeking, but I can tell you that you were chosen by God for a reason, we all were. But before you ask me anymore questions, I will ask you to let me hold your hands."

Elizabeth looked confused but slowly held out her hands, and Lydia took them and closed her eyes. The events that her vision recorded sickened and saddened her to the core. She felt the loneliness, the love, and the anger that filled the young woman's soul, and most of all, the lack of faith that had caused her to do what she did. The vision lasted longer than any of her previous visions, and as it faded, another vision took its place. Lydia knew the Holy Spirit had given her this vision for a purpose.

Opening her eyes, she stared into Elizabeth's face and felt such love and sadness she wanted to put her arms around the young woman but remained seated where she was.

"What is it? What were you doing?" Elizabeth began to feel the fear rising up again, and Lydia quickly tried to reassure her. The last thing Lydia wanted was for the girl to not trust her. It was imperative that she trust and believe what she was told.

"Elizabeth, I have been given a gift, and with this gift comes a commission. I am to help you find peace and to understand the consequences of the decisions you made during your life on earth."

"If you're asking me to confide in you the story of my life, I must tell you I have no desire to go over it again. My memories haunt me without ceasing, and I am unable to speak of them." Elizabeth bowed her head and the slump of her shoulders attested to the burdens she carried.

"Then listen to me, please. I know your father was a minister and your mother a kind, loving, quiet woman. They are buried here in Gable Cemetery as you were. You became a school teacher and lived a simple life until the day you found Abram laying in the road." Lydia was praying that these words would open a dialogue between them.

Horrified, Elizabeth stared at the woman sitting beside her and said, "How, how could you know these things?"

"Remember I told you I had been given a gift? This is my gift. I am able to envision your life. You don't have to tell me what occurred. I know what happened with you and Abram."

The words hung in the air between them, and for a moment, Lydia thought Elizabeth would bolt and run, instead, hanging her head, she sat silently, defeated and ashamed.

Lydia felt such compassion for this poor creature that, unable to control herself, she slid closer and impulsively put her arms around the broken woman and held her as she would have her own child.

Finally lifting her head, Elizabeth pulled away and said, "What happens now? You know the sins I have committed. Are you the one who will send me on to hell, or is hell where I have been all these years?"

"No, I definitely am not sending anyone to hell. But we will speak of all things and hopefully come to an understanding. I don't know what the outcome will be. I only know I am to here to help you, not hurt you. We are no longer alone and that's something, isn't it?"

Elizabeth nodded her head in agreement. Lydia was right. They were no longer alone. She felt less frightened and was beginning to believe that this strange woman beside her would help her to move on to whatever awaited her, assuming this was not her final destiny.

The two women walked the grounds side by side, both unaware of the protective angels that followed them. Their protectors slew any demons that foolishly came close, allowing Elizabeth to think clearly without the influence of the demonic legions, for the first time since she had arrived here, in over 150 years.

"Elizabeth, do you not realize that the comfort you offered Abram was credited to you as a great kindness? Abram was right when he said that God sent him to you that he might experience love for the first time in his life." The question shocked Elizabeth, but as she thought it through, she allowed herself to consider the possibility.

"Then God was looking out for Abram?"

"Of course, but not only for Abram but for you as well. You lost your faith when both of your parents died. Whether or not you admitted it to yourself, you blamed God for taking them from you. Elizabeth, God loves you, and there was a time when you believed in that love. If He did not love you, beyond your comprehension, then you would not have been sent here to relive your life and hopefully see that He always had a plan for you."

"You're trying to tell me that if I had not leaped off that barn beam, there was a life for me without Abram?"

"Yes, and not a continuation of what you had settled for, but a life rich with blessings and joy."

"I don't see how that could be possible. Abram was my life."

"You forget, nothing is impossible with the Heavenly Father. Will you listen if I tell you of the vision that the Holy Spirit gave me when I was holding your hands in the church?"

"I don't know if I can bear to hear what you will tell me." Elizabeth stared down at the ground afraid of what was coming.

"Let's go back to the church. I always find peace when I am there."

They walked to the church side by side, no longer strangers, growing in their knowledge of each other, one a leader and the other beginning to believe this sister had been sent by God himself.

Sitting down on one of the few sturdy remaining pews, Lydia took Elizabeth's hand again and began to talk. "On that Sunday before you took your life, do you remember how you felt energized? You were able to do all the things you had planned without growing weary. And on Monday, before you stepped into the barn, you stood in the yard and lifted your head and smelled the sweet air of early morning."

Elizabeth was stunned at the recounting of those moments. Lydia truly had the gift of visions. She nodded her head. She remembered well each minute leading up to that final act.

"As you balanced on the beam, you were not alone. God assigned an angel to you before your birth, but your loss of faith had diminished his ability to protect you. He tried, not only to save you but there was someone else there with you and he tried to save her as well."

Elizabeth looked confused; there was something wrong with Lydia's vision. No one else was there; she was alone as she stood on the beam. She shook her head and was going to tell Lydia that she had made a mistake, but before she could voice her thoughts, Lydia spoke again.

"You not only took your life that day, but the life of the baby daughter you carried in your womb."

19

"No, no, no! You're wrong! You have to be wrong!" Elizabeth's cries filled the small church as Lydia sat still beside her and waited for the shock of the news to abate.

"Please, please, tell me you're wrong, you must have made a mistake. Lydia, help me..." She rose to her feet in a rush and then quickly dropped to her knees on the plank floor.

"Oh god, oh god! What did I do? Forgive me, Father, I am so sorry."

Lydia reached down and drew her up to sit once more on the pew beside her. There were no words to comfort, no words that could change what had been done. But she drew the grieving woman to her and held her shaking body close.

Elizabeth allowed herself to be held in the arms of this special woman and cried out in her misery. And this time, tears fell from her eyes and flowed in a healing stream until she was empty.

They sat together without words and let God surround them with His love, and gradually, His peace lifted Elizabeth to a new awareness of the grace and forgiveness that was for her, if she would simply accept it. Lydia remained silent waiting for word of what was to happen next. It came in the appearance of Hebron complete with the aura of light that surrounded him like the first time she had seen him.

Lydia rose from the pew and taking Elizabeth's hand drew her up beside her and said softly, "My dear, I want to introduce you to someone." Turning Elizabeth around to face the powerful angel standing behind her, she said, "This is Hebron. He is a mighty warrior angel, and he has been with me since the day I was born."

Elizabeth was shocked, but nothing this woman said or did surprised her now. Staring up at Hebron, she tried not to be frightened in the presence of this amazing creature. She had no doubts that Hebron was indeed who Lydia said he was. She started to drop to her knees in front of him, but Hebron quickly stopped her and kindly admonished her that he was a servant and not to be worshipped; worship was reserved for the Holy One alone. Looking down at her upturned face, he smiled and said, "You have had many things shown to you today, and I know it has been difficult for you, but it is time for you to meet another."

And with that Barael made himself visible, complete with the snow white aura, which was very impressive to his charge. Standing beside Hebron, the two heavenly beings made quite an impression. "Elizabeth, this is Barael, he has been with you since before you were born, and now that you have reaffirmed your faith with our Almighty God, he has been restored to his full strength."

Barael, eager to speak directly to his charge, said, "Elizabeth, I was there when you were born in the south bedroom, when you suckled at your mother's breast, when you took your first steps and said your first words. I know you well, and I am with you now to finish the plan that the Holy Father has set in motion."

Elizabeth gazed up at him and had the distinct feeling that she had always known this creature in front of her. For the first time in her life and these years of her death, Elizabeth felt secure, safe, knowing that God had never abandoned her; forgiveness was hers, and this mighty angel would help her complete the plan that God had for her. She was ready.

Hebron turned his attention to Lydia and said, "It is time for you to meet the next lost soul. You will proceed at your own pace, of course, but be aware that time is running out, and Lucifer will soon be sending his demonic warriors to come for us. All of us! Now there are two of us at full strength but two more wait for you to complete the plan."

Lydia felt the full weight of her responsibility and was eager to begin. Elizabeth and Barael would be leaving her alone to continue her quest, showing themselves when they were needed, but for now, Lydia was again on her own. She followed Hebron to the far northeast corner of the cemetery, and as they approached, she saw the figure of a young man. Looking up at Hebron, she asked, "What is this one's name?"

His name is Jeffrey, and he is as lost as Elizabeth. Pray before you speak, you will need all the heavenly help you can get." And with those words, Hebron was gone. She no longer felt alone when he was not in her sight. She knew she had only to call his name and he would be at her side.

She turned her attention to the man leaning against a tree staring beyond the grounds. It reminded her of the all the times she, too, had stared beyond the crumbling rock fence pondering why she was here. Quietly, she approached him until she was standing close enough to see that he wore a prison uniform and his head was shaved. "Oh my, this young fellow must have quite a tale to tell." With that thought in mind, she bowed her head and prayed for divine guidance and wisdom.

Feeling acutely aware that she had God's blessing, she spoke to the figure in front of her, "Hello, Jeffrey." As with Elizabeth, Lydia spoke softly trying not to startle him.

He spun around and immediately went into a stance ready to fight. His eyes were wide with surprise and fear, his head swaying side to side to see all around him as if he expected to be surrounded. He saw only a young woman standing fifteen feet in front of him. She remained as still as a statue, staring back at him. Both froze in place, waiting for the other to make the first move.

Lydia made the first advance. She took one step in his direction and said, "Jeffrey, don't be afraid. My name is Lydia, and I am here to help you." Without moving closer, she waited for him to absorb her words. He stared at her as if she were a strange animal he had never seen before. Knowing how shocking it was for him to actually see another human being after so many years, she patiently waited for him to find his voice.

"Who are you?" His voice was loud and deep as if trying to frighten her from trying to do him harm.

"My name is Lydia," she reminded him. "I'm not here to cause you harm, Jeffrey. You can trust me. I know you have been here for a long time. So have I. We just couldn't see each other."

"What do you want with me?" He made no move toward her and stayed in a half-crouched position as if ready to defend himself from whatever came at him.

Lydia wasn't exactly sure what she should do next, but she decided she would stay where she was and hope he would make a move to get closer to her. "I would like to talk with you if you will let me. It has been lonely since I arrived here, and I'm happy to be able to have someone to talk with." She finished talking with a smile on her face and what she hoped was a friendly expression.

It must have swayed him a little, for he cautiously rose from his crouch, stood upright, and stared at her with a mix of curiosity and distrust. "How long have you been here?" he asked her in a more normal voice.

"I'm not sure. I know it's been many years because of the different seasons that have come and gone."

Nodding his head as if to tell her he understood, he said, "I don't know how long I've been here either, but it must be half of eternity by now."

Lydia could not help but laugh at his words, and her laughter caused him to smile ruefully. "It's been so long since I've heard someone laugh I'd almost forgotten what it sounded like."

"Jeffrey, would you walk with me awhile? Perhaps we could go to the church and sit for a spell?"

He thought on it and then, making up his mind, nodded his head and cautiously approached her. He was tall, maybe a little over six feet, and young, if she had to guess, she figured he had to have been in his early twenties. She smiled up at him and turned to lead them across the grounds to the church.

"I spend time in the church, not a lot, but when I go there, it reminds me of my mother." The confession surprised Lydia, and she was beginning to think that Jeffrey was not as tough as he tried to be.

They did not speak again until they were seated inside the church. Lydia sat down in the middle of the pew, and Jeffrey plopped down at the far end as if to put as much distance as possible between them. She tried not to smile at his reluctance to get too close to her and began their conversation. "I'll tell you how I came to be here if you would like."

Jeffrey scooted around until he was facing her and nodded for her to go ahead.

"All right, I died the night of my one hundred second birthday party, which must have been somewhat disconcerting to those who showed up to help me celebrate." Lydia paused and chuckled at the thought.

But Jeffrey was not amused. "Are you making fun of me? I may be stupid, but I know you can't be over a hundred! You trying to make me look like a fool?"

She could see how upset he was and quickly reassured him. "No, of course not. I tell you I was completely surprised when I got here and had been turned into my former self. Before I died, I was unable to walk or do anything for myself. It was a terrible, miserable life for many years."

He was staring at her with a skeptical look on his face, but she stared him down, and finally, he seemed to accept that maybe it could have been possible after all; she was sitting here talking to him and only a little while ago, he would have thought that would have been impossible.

She decided not to bring Hebron into the conversation just yet, but to get to know Jeffrey better before telling him they were part of a plan devised by the Creator of the universe, a plan of the utmost importance. She started the conversation again by explaining what she remembered of her trip here.

"I felt like I was falling into a deep black abyss and the next thing I knew, I was inside this capsule, a sort of spinning vortex that was in complete darkness."

Jeffrey interrupted her, "I don't know what a vortex is, but were you scared?"

"No, it was surprisingly peaceful, and I was just getting accustomed to it when there was this blinding light. Everything shattered into a million pieces, and I was dropped in the middle of Gable Cemetery."

"I don't know how I got here. I just woke up and here I was." He spoke haltingly as if how he happened to be here was a complete mystery, which of course, it was.

He was not much of a talker, but Lydia felt that it was time to give him an idea of why they were able to see and talk with each other.

"Jeffrey, I have been given a gift, which enables me to have visions of people and that is why I was brought here. When I arrived, I spent a lot of time reliving my life until I had faced it all, the good and the bad. After I saw that, all the decisions I made during my life had consequences, both the ones I made on my own and the ones that I took to the Father and laid at His feet. I was able to view my life in its entirety and now I believe I may be able to aid you to come to grips with why you are here."

Jeffrey looked like the idea of being examined was not going to be accomplished without dissention on his part. She was quick to reassure him. "There is nothing that you have to do or say, but would you let me hold your hands for a few minutes?"

Looking skeptical, he slowly held out his hands toward her, and she clasped them gently. She was no longer sitting in the church with Jeffrey but seeing his entire life pass before her eyes. She experienced the joy of his mother and father when they realized they would have a child, and the happiness that filled their home when he was born. Lydia was no longer aware of her surroundings or of time as it passed. Sitting in the pew holding Jeffrey's hands, she lived every moment of his life, feeling the love that encircled him as he grew up, the moments when he failed to listen to their admonishments and followed his own desires.

The woman who gave birth to him had prayed fervently for her son from the day he was born until the day she died. Lydia walked beside him during his early years when he looked forward to Sundays, when he loved hearing the pastor's sermons, and the day he felt the Holy Spirit calling him to dedicate his life to the Heavenly Father. There was joy, for a time, as mother and son worshipped together, but the lack of participation from the father he loved gradually dulled and finally diluted the enthusiasm he had felt in the beginning.

Lydia could feel his reluctance to continue to worship a God he could not see, a God his own father had no relationship with. When Jeffrey became the butt of his friends' jokes, friends who made fun of him for always being in church on Sundays, his decision to turn away from the God his mother loved was an easy one.

She felt his anger and his disappointment with himself the day he walked to town and stood outside the school grounds feeling lost and unworthy, saw his hands grab the bike that set everything in motion. She was beside him when his heart was racing and rivulets of sweat ran down his face as he hid inside the house where he had grown up. Her own heart raced as Sheriff Langer's voice called Jeffrey to come out. She watched, horrified as he lost all reasoning and overcome with fear his mind shut down as he reached over the door jamb and took down his father's rifle. She saw the blank stare on his face as his finger twitched, and the gun exploded in his hands, and the smell of gunpowder filled the air. Smoke rose from the barrel, grey and swirling around them.

She was with him through the trial, his isolated years in prison, and finally, the walk down the hallway toward the chair that would end his life. Her vision did not end until he had taken his last breath.

Shaking her head as if to clear it, she became aware she was still holding Jeffrey's hands. She didn't know how long it had taken, but he was staring patiently at her as if waiting for her to start whatever it was she did.

20

Hebron and Barael became instantly alert to a difference in the atmosphere. Sensing their comrades' uneasiness, Aaron and Orion lifted their eyes to the sky.

Gable Cemetery was miles from the nearest city lights. The millions of stars were clearly visible, and the full moon afforded the only illumination of the grounds and headstones, but light was unnecessary as the eyes of demons and their angel enemies were capable of seeing even in the deepest darkness.

Dark, swirling clouds began rolling in from the west. The lightning zigzagged vertically across the dark sky seconds before peels of thunder announced the storm that was rapidly and unfalteringly headed for Gable Cemetery. The storm was gaining in intensity, and the wind had picked up quickly. The wind brought with it the stench of evil to the nostrils of all four of the mighty warriors. They were acutely sensitive to this smell; it was much stronger than the putrid, aridic, odor emitted by the common demons recently destroyed by Aaron's sword. This was a heavy, suffocating stench announcing the imminent invasion of a large regiment of Lucifer's powerful warriors.

Hastily, Hebron signaled for Barael and Orion to guide their charges into the church where Lydia and Jack continued to sit on one of the wooden pews.

Barael had made himself visible to Elizabeth since the moment he first appeared to her. He had become closer and closer to his

153

charge as he watched her grow in faith and acceptance. Elizabeth's journey, with the Holy Spirit as her guide, was swift and ever deepening into total obedience. She was at peace and as she worshipped. She praised her Holy Father with gratitude for this amazing warrior, her very own angel, who was forever at her side.

Orion, unable to materialize himself before Jack, used his majestic wings to gently but surely propel Jack toward the church. And the storm that was approaching helped convince his charge that the church was a welcoming place to be. He had been through many storms, both summer and ice storms, along with frozen ground covered with inches of snow, and it had never bothered him before. But this time, there was something strangely different that made him want to be inside the church.

When all of the charges were safely inside, the four angels walked through the walls to stand at each side of the church. Hebron took his stance at the north entrance in front of the old wooden doors. Barael drifted through the back and stood guard at the east side. Orion and Aaron took their places on the north and south sides respectively, thereby forming a perimeter surrounding the church. Their hands gripped the hilts of their swords in preparation for what was to come. The magnitude of the situation was not lost on the four mighty warriors.

Hebron could not help but wish that Lydia would quickly finish with Jeffrey, allowing Aaron to be restored to his full power. They would desperately need his strength tonight. It was doubtful that the army of demons coming toward them would be Lucifer's most powerful, but he and his comrades would be woefully outnumbered. Taking a deep breath, he calmed himself with the knowledge that Michael always knew the plans of the enemy. The spies who lingered among the filthy demons were the bravest of all the angels, at least in his mind.

The great archangel Michael, relying on those very messengers who stealthily reported to him, had formed plans of his own. Calling together a large number of soldier angels, he gave his orders, and each warrior obeyed without question.

These angels had persevered through many battles, and the four angel warriors stationed below were held in highest regard. These soldiers of God considered it a privilege to fight beside them. Furtively, they dove downward through the firmament and without a sound, dropped to earth around Gable Cemetery. They made their way secretly, silently, without drawing the attention of the constant presence of demons who were singularly focused on the cemetery.

They came two or three at a time. Occasionally, four floated down through the clouds like leaves falling from a tree. Some hid themselves amid the brush, others behind boulders and trees. Still others dove through the upper ground levels and remained just below the surface. Those that chose to hide above ground used their huge wings to wrap around themselves until they were all but invisible. There was no sound as the army of God's angels continued to amass around the tiny cemetery unseen by the hordes of red eyed grotesque creatures that were focused on the plot of ground that held something significant to Almighty God. The silent warrior angels were mindful that every demon was an abomination to be destroyed.

The seasoned warrior angels were so successful in their subterfuge that even Aaron, Hebron, Barael, and Orion were unaware of their presence, just as Michael had ordered.

The Holy Spirit had been doing his job as well. The earthly saints were being convicted that prayers were needed, fervent, drop to their knees kind of prayers. And drop to their knees they did. All over the world—from Asia to Africa, the Americas, and Europe—saints bowed down with eyes closed, arms raised, beseeching their Heavenly Father, for what they did not know exactly, but their faith and obedience was all that was needed. They may not have known why they were being asked to pray, but they heeded the Holy Spirit and their impassioned prayers continued. And strength poured throughout the heavenly realm preparing the warriors for battle.

The prayers of God's earthly children, who devoutly studied the last book of His Holy Word, Revelation, recognized the signs that Scripture defined. The graphic words that described the events leading up to the end of the world as they knew it, words meant only for this generation that would recognize and understand the dire warnings being read. The faithful saints knew that soon the Rapture would be forthcoming. Revelation… warning words to His remnant. This remnant, either in solitude, or in small groups all over the earth prayed and kept prayers coming. And their prayers were the strength surging through the warrior angels throughout the dominion of heaven.

Even with the slow erosion of human decency, the falling away of organized religions, the return of the days of Sodom and Gomorrah, there still remained a remnant of believers. Throughout all of history, God has always preserved a remnant of His own. The prayers of the remnant were sorely needed for a battle that would set in motion the Great War that was to come. The war to fulfill the prophesies of His Holy word.

21

Jeffrey was staring intently at Lydia as she released his hands and clasped her own tightly in her lap. She closed her eyes and beseeched guidance from the Heavenly Father and then, feeling strength and wisdom flowing over her, she spoke to Jeffrey.

"I have been given a gift I never asked for, but God has chosen me to use it for His Glory and to aide you to the answers you have longed for. Jeffrey, while holding your hands, God revealed to me the full account of your life."

"What are you talking about?" He was looking at Lydia as if he might bolt and run to get away from this mad woman.

"I saw the joy on your mother and father's faces the day you were born. They loved you as much as any child could be loved, and on that day, your mother lifted you up and dedicated you and your life to God."

Jeffrey's eyes were round and startled, he began to shake his head. "This is crazy! It's nuts. I don't know what's goin' on, but I know this is just plumb impossible!"

"You were born on a farm, the farm that your dad inherited when your grandparents passed away. Your mother was raised in the city by influential people who disowned her when she married your father."

Jeffrey sat silent, staring at her with a look of total confusion on his face.

"Your mother had the most beautiful hair I have ever seen, and your father loved her very much."

At this comment, Jeffrey froze and began to pay close attention to what this extraordinary woman was saying. His head was spinning, and his heart, beating rapidly in his chest, caused his breathing to be labored and shallow. He was still unconvinced, even a little scared, but for now, he was willing to hear what she had to say.

Lydia saw that her last words had had a profound effect on the young man, and now he was listening carefully to what she was saying.

"There were times as you were growing up when they differed on how to help you grow into the man they hoped you would become."

"You can say that again."

"They did the best they could. You were loved and wanted. Do you remember the Sunday that you were in church sitting beside her and you felt the call to surrender your life to the Lord?"

He nodded his head as the memory washed over him. "I was scared to get up and walk down to the front. It seemed like a whole mile down there before I made it to Preacher Dan. He put his arms around me, and I began to sob like I was a baby, but I wasn't bawling because I was sad but because I felt so happy."

"I know, and when you asked God to come into your life, that's exactly what He did. And when you were baptized that day, the Holy Spirit entered into you, and they have never stopped loving you." Laying a comforting hand upon his shoulder, she continued, "Jeffrey, your name was written in the Book of Life. You belong to the Lord, and that is why you are here."

"That can't be true. You don't know the thing I did. No one could love me after all the pain I caused." He dropped his head unable to look at Lydia's face or accept the kindness showing in her eyes.

"That's not true Jeffrey. God forgives us when we ask for forgiveness, and I can tell you that Sherriff Langer's wife and his grown children forgave you long ago. The only one who has not forgiven you is yourself. Jeffrey, you are more important than you can imagine. Your mother, and towards the last of his life, your father, prayed on their knees for you to come back to God."

Looking at him to see how he was accepting what she said, she continued, "There are others here, like yourself, who made mistakes during their lives. But also like you, they are being assigned the most important task ever given to God's most loved creation since the beginning of time."

Fear caused his body to quake. He was terrified to hear what was coming. He had always failed at whatever he tried to do, and if this was as important as she was acting like it was, then boy, they were all in a heap of trouble. Big trouble!

"You must listen very carefully, Jeffrey, so much depends on you. When I came here, time ceased to exist, and I was bombarded with visions of my life over and over again, until finally I could see that all the decisions I had made had consequences that reached out and impacted not only myself but those around me. I made a decision to follow Jesus when I was younger than you were, and I stayed close to him, growing in the word all my life."

She looked sharply to see if he was buying any of this and was pleased to see that he was hanging on every word. "I knew there were angels assigned to each one of us, but it was only after the visions of my life ceased that Hebron allowed himself to be seen by me."

"Wait, are you telling me that you can see an angel?"

"Yes, and his name is Hebron, and he has explained why we are here. He told me there are three names left to be entered into the Book of Life, and those three rejected the Lord. You are one of those three. It is almost time for the Rapture, but until you all decide, on your own, to open your hearts to Christ, and repent, the Rapture cannot come to pass. The world is quickly turning into madness, and soon, God will have his fill of evil upon it. You three hold the key to opening the doors of heaven and signaling the Rapture to begin."

Jeffrey sat with mouth agape, shaken to his core but believing each word that he heard.

"What can I do, what can I do?"

Jeffrey felt a fierce desire to do something right this once, just *this* once to not fail.

Great sobs began to rack his body, and unable to control himself, he fell to the floor. Lying prostrate on the ages old oak floor, he continued to weep; his sobs filling the room until at last his tears dried up. Trying to speak, drawing air deep into his lungs, he raised his stricken face toward heaven and began to express himself in slow faltering words torn from deep within.

"Father, forgive me. I know I don't deserve it, but I truly am so sorry. I will do anything you ask of me. I want to try to make up for all the terrible things I did. Please, please, forgive me!"

At his words, the room filled with light despite the storm that was drawing ever closer. Lydia looked up to see Hebron standing beside the most amazing creature she had ever seen. He was larger than Hebron, if that were possible, and she thought that if he were to spread his enormous wings, what was left of the roof of the tiny church would be blown off.

Blinded by the intensity of the pure white light that filled the room, Jeffrey staggered to his feet, and with one hand held over his eyes to shield them, he reached for Lydia with his other hand.

"It's all right, Jeffrey, I want you to meet Hebron. And this other astounding angel of God is, I believe, your own personal angel who has been with you since the moment you were born."

The light dimmed to a more tolerable level as Hebron took a step closer, and, smiling at Jeffrey, said, "This is Aaron, one of the mightiest of all the warrior angels. He has fought more battles against the most powerful of Lucifer's demons than any of us!"

Aaron quickly pulled Hebron back and addressed Jeffrey himself.

"Never mind what Hebron said. Sometimes, he forgets himself. It is true that I have been with you all your life, even after your death, I have been constantly by your side. When you withdrew from the Master, I no longer had your faith to give me strength to slay the demons that surrounded you. But now, with your faith restored, I am at my full strength and a battle is about to begin."

Turning to Hebron, Lydia asked, "Is it near?"

Nodding his head, he calmly told her, "They are close, and their numbers fill the sky. Tonight with Aaron able to fight at his peak, we have a chance. They are coming to destroy not only us, but all of you as well. They still do not know the importance of you four to Almighty God, but they know something is happening here that causes their master to suspect it may be more important than even he realized."

Chuckling out loud, Hebron continued, "And nothing makes the leader of the demonic legions madder than to be made a fool of."

Barael and Elizabeth suddenly appeared, shocking Jeffrey at the sight of not only a strangely dressed woman but another of the majestic angels. This one was dressed exactly as Hebron and Aaron, long white cassocks, with sashes at their waist holding the scabbards for their swords. Only the grips of their swords were visible, and they were huge, attesting to the size of the weapon that each angel would use in battle.

Aaron quickly introduced them to Jeffrey and taking charge directed them to remain inside the church.

"We don't have much time. They are almost upon us. Do not leave the church for any reason. Gather together and pray as you never have before. We will need the prayers of many saints to survive this night."

Lydia looked at Hebron, and taking hold of his sleeve, as if to detain him, asked, "What about the last lost soul? Is there no time for me to meet with him?"

"No, but he is here inside the church. He cannot see you or Elizabeth or Jeffrey. But he is here, and hopefully, he will remain inside for if he should venture outside these walls, I don't know that we can protect him without endangering the rest of you. This is the only place that you may be safe and where we will protect you with our lives. His angel will be the fourth that guards over you tonight."

And with those words, they left through the walls. Jeffrey stared for a moment but decided that, with everything he had learned, nothing would surprise him again. Turning back to the women, he gave Elizabeth a smile, which she returned. They stood for a moment, staring at each other and trying to absorb what they had heard. Jeffrey mumbled, "I didn't think anything would make me afraid again since I'm dead, but this is going to be a long night." He couldn't help noticing the color of her hair, a deep auburn he had never seen before.

Lydia broke the spell, and taking charge had them drop to their knees, and the three saints began to pray as they had never prayed before. They prayed aloud, one after the other, unaware of their surroundings and not knowing what would happen to them during this night. Fear was no longer in their minds, only great love for the Savior and the Heavenly Father. Their faith grew as the hours passed, and their voices grew as one, lifted up to the heavens and heard loud and clear by all the Heavenly Host.

PART 6

The Trumpet Sounds

For our struggle is not against flesh and blood, but against the rulers, against the authorities, against the powers of this dark world and against the spiritual forces of evil in the heavenly realms.

—Ephesians 6:10–12

22

There was no unusual activity around the area; nothing could be seen from land or air. The silent angel sentries remained perfectly still, not a sound was made. It appeared the deep shadows had swallowed them as they blended into the forest that surrounded the small cemetery on three sides. They watched the black cloud filled with hordes of Satan's demons, advancing closer to the cemetery.

They witnessed the four veteran warriors emerge from the church and stand ready for the onslaught. But still they remained hidden, waiting, waiting...

The warriors had stood guard many times over the eons of time. But this night, their instincts, honed over the ages, were acutely on edge as the moon shadows danced over the weathered tombstones half hidden by overgrown weeds and thistles. Aaron, an enigmatic expression on his weathered face, knew beyond doubt that tonight would be an epic battle and they could not fail.

Turning his eyes toward the heavens, he stared intently into the darkening sky. The others stood rigidly at attention looking upward as well.

"It's almost time. I feel as if all of heaven is holding its breath," Aaron said softly.

"I feel it, too," Barael said. "It was a very long time ago when I first felt this kind of premonition."

Orion agreed, "I, too, remember that time, when the Holy One created it all, the galaxies, the trillions of stars and suns, and this special planet, which was His favorite. It was a glorious time, and He was so pleased with His creation. We were all one then, filled with worship until Lucifer turned on the Holy of holies and convinced his legions to break away and follow him. In all of eternity, never had there been such chaos in heaven. Nor were there feelings of anger and angst before. The entire heavenly realm cowered at God's anger that day, and we who remained loyal fought the battle of all battles until we defeated Lucifer and brought him and his guilty followers before the throne."

They nodded in agreement as each drew from their memories the egregious time when all of heaven was darkened by the wrath of God's anger.

Hebron picked up the account they had witnessed millions of years before.

"It was the Eocene of earth time, after the first creation, as the Master watched the evolution of matter and creatures develop. But He was not pleased with the results of life form upon His earth. Remember, it was then He destroyed the entire earth with the first flood?"

"But when He restored the earth again, what magnificence we witnessed. In seven earth days, He restored it to its original form and transported such exquisite beauty from heaven itself to reside here. And then the Creator brought all of creation to its knees when He created man, a being with free will who would be capable of loving and worshipping Him. A creation upon whom He could pour out His blessings." Aaron paused, experiencing the painful memory that followed.

Their combined silence hung heavy between them until Barael continued the age-old story. "There was a period of awesome peace when the earth flourished, and the Lord came and had companionship with His created children. Never before or since has there been such joy, both in heaven and upon the earth."

Hebron's deep voice was low as he uttered the thoughts that had plagued him for countless centuries. "I would never question

Almighty God, but when Lucifer and his armies were imprisoned in the lake of fire, there was no strife anywhere in all of the heavens, and harmony reigned throughout. Only when the Master unlocked the gate and released the repugnant, salacious, evil ones and allowed them to come here, to rule over the earth, did the vast ruination begin…" His voice trailed off, and he dropped his head fearful that he had said too much.

"Yes, all of that is true," Aaron replied, "but I have raised this very thought to Michael. He was quick to chastise me for not completely trusting in the Master's wisdom. Our faith must be indestructible for our strength to be at its fullest. And when I was with him the last time, he told me it would all be made clear to us and to all the earthly believers, both alive and dead in Christ who silently wait for the coming of judgment. I know the time is near, and the battle before us will be even greater than the war we fought with Lucifer in heaven! So I ask each of you, do you trust Almighty God without qualm or question?"

Each of the majestic warriors consciously recommitted their full trust and loyalty to their Creator, and in that exact moment, the darkness that surrounded them was pulled apart over their heads, and rays of divine light were around and about them. They basked in the glorious brightness and knew that their Master was pleased with their response. The spell lasted only a millisecond in earth time, but it was enough. They were ready.

Aaron now stood guard at the entrance doors, and Hebron had taken his place at the east side. A strangeness had begun to envelope the area, a sickening heaviness that caused dogs, miles away, to begin howling and stalking fence lines or crawling deeper under porches. Residents came out, shouting and cussing at the four-legged sentries, but something caused the hair on the back of their necks to rise, and uneasy, they quickly withdrew back inside the safety of their houses, turned on lights in every room, and tried to pretend nothing was happening.

Off in the distance, the western section of the sky began to cast an ominous glow across the land, moving ever closer, until Aaron could see hundreds of bright red embers coming toward them and immediately recognized they were the burning eyes of thousands of demons. What had appeared as rolling clouds was actually thick vapor pouring from the nostrils of the grotesque creatures whose scales covered their bodies, their black wings shaking and pulsating until they looked like a rolling sea of evil.

Aaron was beginning to hear the furious guttural, hissing sounds coming from their throats, the sound growing in volume and becoming more distinct as they drew nearer. Their foul and noxious breath filled the air around them with a dark grey mist. Many times, he had slain them as they attempted to attack him with their misshapen, gnarled fingers and razor-sharp yellow talons that curled downward. Drawing himself up to his full height, he prepared to protect those he had been chosen to watch over.

Each angel warrior had the same thoughts. "Keep them at a distance with our swords, or they will overpower us with sheer numbers. And what they will do to the souls inside the church is unthinkable!"

Aaron's voice rang out as he gave the order. "Draw your swords!"

The enormous cloud of demons filling the sky as far as could be seen was almost upon them.

Aaron's garments began to glow with an ethereal white light. The cassocks of Hebron, Orion, and Barael also began to shine with a brilliance that lit up the field of battle around the small church. At the sound of Aaron's war cry, the earth shook. They drew their swords as one. The gigantic swords blazed with a dazzling light so bright it blinded the demons on the front lines, destroying their bodies like bolts of lightning. Their ear-piercing screams of terror erupted from their hideous throats, as they plummeted to the earth and disintegrated into dust, evaporating into a macabre mist that blended into the air.

The atmosphere had changed. A penetrating cold was moving across the cemetery and then the onslaught was upon them. The noise was maddening; shrieks, cursing, and blaspheming filled the air. The great warrior angels moved with such velocity they seemed to be a blur. Their massive swords flashed and dipped, ripping bodies and slashing throats with precision. Warrior demons screamed in agony as they died and disintegrated in a hideous grey mist that carried their stench upward.

The frontline legions were quickly abolished, but their numbers were unending and as one would die, ten more would swoop down upon the tiring angels. The din was so loud the humans inside the church rose from their knees and stared at each other in alarm. They drew together tightly, prepared to fight for as long as they could. Jeffrey pushed the women behind him and dropped down into his fighting stance as he had when he first arrived at the prison.

Orion fought with sheer determination, but with the lack of faith from his charge, he drew weary, and sensing the weakness in him, the demons surrounded him and increased their attack. He was battered and beaten to his knees until he could no longer hold the huge sword and five of the twittering demons drew closer for the kill. An air of desolation came over him as their talons and fangs tore at his flesh and the demons, squealing with victory, left him for finished, his body ripped apart, as they entered the chapel through the windows at the rear of the church as several more dropped down from the uncovered rafters of the roof.

Fear engulfed the children of God at their first sight of the hideous demons. The foul odor radiating from them filled the room and caused the four to be overcome with nausea.

The devils flew into the room, pushing and shoving, angling to be first to sink their claws and fangs into these souls, so precious to the Great Jehovah. Knowing Lucifer would reward them heartily for tormenting these four, they quickly surrounded them in a homicidal rage and began to dive and dig at them, torturing them until their screams echoed off the walls.

Jack Simmons was unaware there were others like him in the church. The demons' attack on him was less penetrating, as he was still swimming in a sea of confusion and doubts. He felt an overpowering sense of mourning and hopelessness as the fiends tormented him from all sides. But for Lydia, Elizabeth, and Jeffrey, the demons that filled the room were intent on brutalizing and assaulting them before bringing them to their leader as lambs to the slaughter.

Pervasive evil filled the room as slithering, leering, demons of lust, complacency, anger, jealousy, murder, confusion, doubt, and vilest of all, the demon of hate, which poisoned minds until love was driven out. He carried a black sword, was dressed in a black cassock, his face was gnarled and contorted with hate for all mankind and for these four in particular. He was the mightiest demon in the room and determined to bring these souls to Satan on his own. The squabbling and fighting between the furious smaller demons and the larger more seasoned demon lessened the attack on the four.

Aaron was driven to his knees, his strength ebbing. He continued to slay with his sword, but his enemies could sense his defenses were growing low and more and more they came at him, darting and diving, staying just out of his reach, but tiring him to his limits.

Hebron and Barael, fighting on opposite sides of the church, were in the same quandary. They slew masses of the hideous creatures, but it seemed to be an endless battle, and now they could hear the cries of their charges coming from inside, the chapel and realized the demons had entered and were terrorizing the souls that belonged to God.

The mighty warriors had fought valiantly and killed untold numbers of Satan's soldiers... just enough, the end of the horde could be seen on the horizon. Lucifer had sent more than he thought was needed to rid this place of these troublesome angels and the charges they watched over. He commanded them to kill the angels of the Lord and bring the souls of the four to him. He had plans for these four.

Above the clamoring noises of the fierce battle, a sound reverberated from the heavens... the all-encompassing sound of a trumpet made of a ram's horn, a deep thundering sound that had never before been heard on earth. For a split second, it caused all to freeze in place and shocked the victorious demons who had already begun to celebrate. They glanced furtively at each other and began to hiss and drool at this strange sound. For a moment, nothing moved, and in that moment, the great archangel Gabriel blew again on his mighty shofar. It was the signal for which the warrior angels had been waiting.

They came in rapid speed from under the earth, behind the trees, from wherever they had hidden themselves, and surrounded the entire demonic legion. They flew into the horde sending them tumbling to their deaths. Weapons flashed as they systematically slew all of the demons, not one was spared. The cries of the dying, the shrill begging and pleading of the last of the living finally ceased.

Only the demons inside the church remained alive. They shook with fear as they heard the dying cries of their comrades. Knowing if they were to flee, there was no chance of escaping, so they waited for death to come to them and wailed and screamed, as if their cries would save them. Groveling pitifully, they slithered across the floor, seeking a place in which to hide.

Outside, Aaron drew himself to his feet, and reeling from exhaustion, careened into the wooden doors of the church sending them slamming to the floor, with their hinges hanging broken and useless. His rage at what Lucifer's demonic henchmen had done to these loved ones of the Heavenly Father consumed him with anger as never before. He no longer felt fatigued, and the sword at his side was raised high above his head as he brought it down again and again until only one demon remained alive.

Hate stared at the warrior standing before him and knew he would not survive this battle, but he flew with lightning speed directly into Aaron, fighting with the weapons he had. His bared fangs latched onto Aaron's shoulder, and his long pointed talons reached for the eyes of his enemy. He dug in deep until Aaron's other hand grabbed him around his neck and, jerking him away, threw him to the floor. The massive sword came down upon him and severed his ghastly head from his body. It rolled along the floor before disintegrating into a heavy mist that rose to the ceiling and disappeared through the rafters.

They were gone.

23

The squads of warrior angels left as one. Few of their numbers had been lost in battle. Rising up toward the pale morning sun, they silently returned to the heavenly realm where they would prepare for the next battle.

Inside the church, Aaron helped Hebron and Barael check on the four charges before tending to Orion who was the most badly injured. Lying on the ground at the back of the church, he was near death. His breathing was slow and labored; his wounds deep and numerous. One arm was almost severed from his body; his face bore the wounds of their fury, ripped and torn from their fangs and claws; he was almost unrecognizable. The demons who attacked him in a frenzy of rage had been so anxious to get inside they had not stayed to make sure he was dead.

Although he was not at his full strength when the battle began, Orion had fought courageously, sending great numbers of the cowardly demons into oblivion. Aaron lifted him up and carefully carried him inside. There was a hush at the sight of his unmoving body as Aaron gently laid him on a wooden pew. Lydia and the others, though traumatized and wounded themselves, dropped to their knees and bowed their heads to the floor beside him. They prayed as one that Yahweh would heal this protector and faithful servant.

As they prayed, the room became filled with warmth, and radiance emitted from Orion's body as one by one the hideous wounds began to mend. The restorative warmth spread throughout the room soothing their wounds as the Holy Spirit moved softly about, gently touching their ravaged bodies until all were healed.

Orion took a deep breath and slowly drew himself upright on the pew. It was the first time for the three souls to see this angel, and he smiled fondly at them. They drew a collective breath of gratitude for God's mercy as they watched Orion return to his normal self. Although he was still not at full strength, Lydia knew that he would be fully restored later.

Outside, a capricious breeze carried the last remnants of the dead demons' scent away. The sun was shining with barely a cloud in the fall sky.

A poignant refrain drifted in through the windows, and the four angels lifted their heads in unison and smiled at the lustrous melody. They knew what, and who, produced the pleasing sound. It had resonated at different times throughout human history.

Lydia stared questioningly at Hebron and he in turn looked at Aaron. Aaron nodded his head in consent, giving Hebron permission to tell her what made the delicious sound.

"The great archangel Gabriel is here. He is the angel of revelation, and it was he who blew the trumpet summoning our rescuers from their hiding places. Wait here while we speak with him and receive the instructions he has brought."

"I want to see him, too. Hebron, I have read so much about him. It was Gabriel who told Mary of God's plan for her to be the mother of the infant Messiah. I can think of no greater privilege than to see him, except for being in the presence of Jesus and the Father, of course."

"I'm afraid that won't be possible for now. Not until you have all received your resurrected bodies. If you were to look upon him now, you would not enjoy the experience. But soon you will be able to spend all the time with him you want."

Lydia turned away, disappointed but willing to wait, and drew Elizabeth and Jeffrey to her. They consoled each other over what they had experienced and rejoiced at God's grace. Lydia had not forgotten the assignment ahead, and after what they had experienced throughout this long night, the significance of what was expected of her weighed heavily on her heart.

Gabriel stood outside the small chapel as the four angels came toward him. An aura of white and gold surrounded his body; his magnificent wings were closed now. He looked upon these warriors with a deep affection.

Aaron spoke first, "Gabriel, thank you for the rescue. The sound of your mighty horn was most gratifying. We were at the end of our strength. You could not have summoned the warriors at a better time."

"I would have preferred to have summoned them sooner, but it was imperative that every one of Lucifer's demonic soldiers be destroyed. None could be allowed to report back to him what was occurring here. At first, he will assume they have not returned because they are celebrating their victory, but eventually, he will realize they are not going to return. His anger will be immeasurable. The next time he will not send puny warriors, but will personally lead his greatest warriors and a host of demonic creatures to wipe out the souls that are needed to fulfill Jehovah's plan. We have bought more time, precious time, to bring the last soul to Almighty God before it is too late."

"The prayer warriors had best keep praying, for if we run out of time, and Lucifer descends upon us again, the results may not be as satisfying."

Hebron spoke solemnly, and the other three nodded their heads in agreement.

"I know Hebron wasted no time in bringing Lydia and Jack together. It is imperative that he awaken and freely repent and ask for forgiveness. I will leave now and join Michael to prepare for what is to come. I will tell him you are pleased with the battle plans he arranged."

And with those words, the glorious angel spread his massive wings to their fullness and rose into the heavens, leaving behind a trail of color as a beautiful rainbow spread across the sky from horizon to horizon.

Looking at each other, the four angels did not speak. They had no need for words. They were keenly aware that what was to come would be the most colossal event to occur on earth since God created the universes.

Quickly, they entered the church and met with the three souls that so much depended upon.

Barael stood by Elizabeth as Aaron walked to Jeffrey's side. Turning to Lydia, Barael spoke, "We will leave you alone to deal with your next assignment, Lydia." And they quietly left with their charges close to their sides.

A flock of migrating birds flew across the sky heading south as was their custom, a sure sign of an early winter. People across the globe continued with the routines of their daily existence, unaware of the enormity of what had been set in motion. Most all of mankind were so involved in their day-to-day lives that they had no thoughts of the events occurring around them and assumed that tomorrow would be like today, births and deaths causing great joys or deep sorrows. Believing that tomorrow, the sun would rise and set as always.

Lydia stood before Hebron and waited for him to introduce her to the last soul.

"I'm ready, and I'm fully aware there isn't much time, so let's not waste it."

"He's still here in the church. He was unable to grasp what was going on, but he has been shaken, and he is in a state of confusion and fear. Pray for wisdom before you begin. You will need it!"

As was his way, Hebron silently left, and Lydia saw a man standing beside an open window. He wasn't moving; his body was rigid, as he stared out over the grounds.

"Don't be afraid," she spoke softly.

He was so startled, he almost collapsed. Only by grabbing the side of a pew did he manage to keep from falling. Looking around, his eyes settled on Lydia standing beside the altar of the church. The astonishment he felt clearly visible on his face.

"Jack, it's all right. I'm here to help you."

It took him several tries before he could get any sound to come out.

"Who are you? Where did you come from? How do you know my name?"

The questions poured out like a dam had burst inside him.

"My name is Lydia. Like you, when I died, I awakened to find myself here. For a very long time, I did not understand how I got here or why."

"I don't understand any of this, how come I can see and hear you now? Did you just get here?"

"No, like you, I have been here for a long time, but you need to recognize that during our lives, time was important, but here, time has little meaning."

"What are we going to do? I need to know what this is all about."

"That is why I have been sent here. There are two more here that, like you, have been chosen out of all humanity for an extremely important commission. You are needed to fulfill a great promise."

Lydia waited for her words to sink in and for Jack to respond. It didn't take him long.

"What the hell are you talking about, woman? Good grief, now I have lost my mind!" He shook his head as if to clear it and closed his eyes tightly. Opening them, he was disappointed that Lydia still remained in his line of vision.

Smiling sweetly, Lydia walked toward him, sat down on the nearest pew, and motioned for Jack to join her. He hesitated, but finally, deciding his curiosity was greater than his fear, crossed the room and sat down at the end of the pew, leaving a large space between them.

"I'll explain as best I can. It's a fairly long story but feel free to interrupt and ask questions if there is something you don't understand."

Jack nodded and settled back to hear what this unassuming apparition had to say. Besides, he had to admit, it was so good to hear another voice.

"Let's start with me and how I came to be here. I lived a very long life on earth, one hundred and two years to be exact."

Jack's reaction was expected, and Lydia quickly explained, "When we die, we do not remain in the weakened, disabled bodies we had on earth. Our features stay the same, but our bodies are restored to the best that we have been or the way we should have been. Do you understand?"

"You mean the blind can see, and the lame can walk?" Jack said in a mocking voice.

"That's it exactly!"

She had chosen to ignore his disbelief and went on with her story.

"I had been in a nursing home for eight years, unable to speak, or walk, or do anything for myself. My mind was gone, I had lost myself. It was terribly humiliating to need others to take care of my every need…"

Her voice drifted off, remembering that embarrassing time. Shaking her head to clear it of the pictures that flashed before her, she said, "I'm sorry, Jack. I don't normally dwell on those times. But ten days before my death, I suddenly had an awakening of a sort. I knew everyone and could think rationally. Being able to process sounds was marvelous and best of all was when someone touched me. The moment we made contact, I could see—actually see—their entire lives. I knew this gift of visions came from the Heavenly Father, and there was a purpose for it. I had no idea why I had been given a gift such as this, but I knew He had a plan."

Jack was nodding his head like he understood every word this crazy woman was saying, but he was thinking, "Great, I finally have someone with me and she turns out to be a raving maniac."

Lydia could not fail to see the expression on his face but continued, "When I arrived here, the visions became my own, and I relived my life over and over. The visions would not stop, and for a while, they made no sense. I finally realized that throughout my life, every decision I made, large or small, had consequences. Some were simple, but others had a grave impact on those around me."

She paused for breath as Jack began having second thoughts as he listened to this strange woman. The events she was describing mirrored the things that happened to him, and he didn't like where she was going with her story.

He stood up and looked toward the door. Lydia remained sitting very still.

"You can leave if you want to. You can run away and not accept what is waiting for you, but if you do, you will never know peace, or love, or forgiveness. Your decision, Jack."

She held her breath while Jack swayed between fear and his desire to not be alone for all of eternity. She knew it was not time to fully explain why he was here or what was expected of him. He would never be able to stand up to those expectations without the courage that being restored to his Savior and his Holy Father would give him. She waited… and waited, as Jack stood before two doors, she prayed he would select the right one, so much depended on this young man.

And all of heaven waited with her.

24

Jack slowly turned around to face her and dropped limply back onto the pew. He had made a decision; he could not bear to be alone any longer. The isolation he had endured over the decades of time he had been here was not something he could face any longer.

"I don't know where you're going with this, and for sure, I don't know that I can accomplish whatever it is you're alluding to, but let's hear the rest of your story."

Lydia slid closer and raising her hands said, "May I hold your hands?"

Hesitantly, he reached for hers, and instantly, Lydia began her journey experiencing Jack's life, his birth, in a dreary, cheaper than cheap hotel room with busted shades on the one window, and sheets on the rickety bed that had not seen the insides of a washing machine for a fortnight.

The first three and a half years of his life were filled with constant comings and goings of different men. Some earned the name "uncle" for staying around long enough to supply food and a roof over their heads, before tiring of both him and the beautiful woman who was the center of his young life.

And finally, the day that mother and son walked the last few miles from the two-lane highway where they had been dropped off by the latest of many truck drivers, walked until Jack's chubby legs gave out on him, and the redheaded woman he adored carried him the last mile to the weathered white farm house.

The elderly couple loved him from the instant they opened their front door and saw their runaway daughter standing forlornly before them. The child on her hip would become their reason for living. They in turn became Jack's security, his safety, and his guides to a Heavenly Father.

These loving grandparents were the only truly stable thing Jack had in the early years of his life. And the heartbreaking anguish they felt at watching mother and son leave for a home they felt would be one more mistake, one more thing, for them to endure with their only child.

Lydia witnessed the years of constant prayers for this grandson whom they loved and fretted over. She saw his contentment at being grounded in a loving family, excelling at school, surrounded by friends up until that fateful day.

She felt his nervousness as he climbed into the car and instinctively knew there was something horribly wrong. She watched him as he silently rode beside his mother, who ignored him, as she drove to a fateful meeting she was dreading but did not know how to avoid. The endless minutes they sat in the parked car on the isolated road until the pickup came toward them and stopped alongside.

The fear that tore at his heart, as the strange man leaned down to look inside the car and was so angered at sight of the boy whose back was braced against the car door. The madness began when the man took a step back, yelled obscenities, and drawing a gun from his jacket pocket, leveled the barrel at his mother and fired the weapon. The sound echoing over and over as her blood splattered throughout the car and Jack froze, unable to move.

The minutes dragged by as he stared at her body. Her beautiful hair became matted with blood, and her eyes stared straight ahead as Jack waited beside her throughout that agonizingly long night.

Lydia experienced the years after the horrific episode and how it molded his thinking and his unspoken anger at a Holy God who would let such a thing happen. She saw the beautiful young woman who grew to love him and believed that her love would be enough to drive away the demons that surrounded him. And, sadly, Lydia watched him dive deeper and deeper into the endless bottles of booze to stop the voices and try to find peace in a vast darkness. It was a treacherous road that brought only a dreadful yearning for total oblivion from his memories, which is exactly what his life became.

She shared his every moment including his last hour when his car slid below the surface of the shadowy pond, when the icy water woke him from his stupor and his agonized screams ricocheted throughout the submerged car as he frantically fought to open the door and escape the swiftly rising water.

She was trembling and breathing heavily when Jack's voice brought her out of her vision. "Lydia! Lydia, are you all right?"

He was staring at her closely, concerned that something was dreadfully wrong with this woman who was the first human contact he had since he awoke here in this lonely cemetery.

She opened her eyes, relieved to be out of this last vision, and extremely troubled at how to proceed. Staring at Jack's face, she knew she must not rely on her own wisdom. Turning her face away from him, she closed her eyes again and, raising her face toward heaven, prayed ardently for guidance, knowing what depended on this man before her.

"Hey, are you okay?" Jack's voice was filled with concern.

Turning back to face him, she nodded her head and comforted him with a wry smile. "I'm all right, Jack. I've had a long vision of your life and experienced the episodes that drove you to the path that led you to destruction."

Jack was not only skeptical, it was obvious he didn't believe a word she had spoken.

"Ah, I see you don't trust me. You haven't believed in anything or anyone for a long time, but most of all, you stopped believing in yourself when your mother was killed!"

She let her last words sink into his consciousness.

His face registered the shock he was feeling at her words. "How could you possibly know what happened that night?"

"Because, I was there with you. My visions allow me to experience all that you experienced. The Lord gave me this gift in order to help you understand what went wrong in your life. Jack, do you believe me now?"

"I don't know… I know I don't want to hear anymore. I don't want to believe you." He was shaking his head back and forth as if that would help him escape her words. His jaw clenched tightly, and he dropped his head, unable to look at her any longer.

Her words pounded at him. "It's time for you to face the truth, and the truth is, it isn't God you have been running from, but yourself. You blame yourself for not trying to do something to save your mother. It's guilt that you tried to drown but, Jack, an ocean of alcohol could not extinguish the burden of guilt you needlessly took upon yourself. You were a child. There was nothing that you could have done that would have changed the outcome of that instant. All of your mother's decisions led up to that moment, and you had nothing to do with it. I witnessed what happened inside the car, and I swear to you, it was not your fault!"

"No, no, no!" He was shaking his head violently, and leaping to his feet, he screamed out, "I should have done something. I could have jumped out of the car and made him come after me, or I could have thrown a fit and made her take us home… I could have done something!"

"No matter what you could have done or should have done, nothing would have stopped this man who believed that he could not live without her. Love can be a wonderful thing, Jack. Or it can be a tool that destroys both of those involved." She hesitated, waiting for her words to be received. "Like the love you had for Sue Ann, but you never believed you were worthy to be loved, and you drove her away deliberately. Whether you believe that or not, it's true."

Silence hung between them as Lydia waited, acutely aware that their time was running out.

Jack seemed frozen in time until his body began to tremble, and a heartbreaking sound escaped from his lips. His sobs became louder and, like she had with the others, Lydia put her arms around him and let him empty himself of all the tragic years of regret.

When he had quieted, she began to speak softly, "Do you remember the feelings you had when you were with your grandparents at the church, when you felt the Holy Spirit leading you to make a decision to follow Jesus? You chose to do just that. Jack, God never turns his face away from a soul that he has called. He assigned an angel to you the moment you were born, for you were destined to be called. Your faith in the Savior is what gave your angel the strength to watch over you and protect you. When you turned your back on God, you severely hampered the ability of your angel to fight Satan's demons that have tortured you throughout your life and continue to attack you even now."

"I have an angel?"

Lydia nodded her head.

"Where is he?"

"Here."

Jack sat very still and turning his head, scanned the room.

"I suppose you can see him?" he whispered.

"No, not yet, but first, it is imperative for you to understand how much the Holy Father loves you. The angel assigned to you is one of the strongest and most revered warriors in the heavenly kingdom."

Lydia rose to her feet, pacing back and forth as she gathered her thoughts. Knowing it was time, she had to tell him now. She began, "Jack, there are two other souls here, who like you, accepted Christ as their Savior during their lives and, also like you, when circumstances confronted them they could not deal with, they turned their backs on God. But He never left them, never ceased to love them without measure. The same as He has always loved you. The time you have been here was His way of giving each of you one last chance to choose to repent and come back to Him. You three are the keys that will set in motion the greatest event the world has ever seen—the Rapture."

The words hung between them. Jack had lost all doubt that this woman was who she said she was, but even believing her, he had a difficult time accepting what she was saying. The enormity of it was beyond his comprehension.

"Why wouldn't God turn His back on someone like me? How could he possibly trust me with something as important as this?"

"He has always chosen those whom the world deems totally unworthy. Always! Those that He chose were incapable of performing amazing feats on their own, but He gave them whatever strengths or wisdom was needed. Each one of them knew without doubt they were powerless without Him. With God, all things are possible. He could have chosen souls who were totally faithful and obedient, but it is the lost sheep, the ones who fall away that are so very important to Him."

Lydia hesitated for a moment and then continued, "One other thing, the Lord has put on my heart to tell you that He heard every prayer lifted up for you by your grandmother and grandfather. They had tremendous faith and love for Him, and they never stopped praying for you. Never ceased pleading for you. The other two lost souls also had loved ones who prayed continually for them."

Jack studied on that for a while, and then asked, "What am I supposed to do now?"

"You must decide whether to give yourself totally to our Heavenly Father or face what comes without Him. It is a decision that only you can make. God refuses to take away free will. You, like all humankind, must choose for yourself."

Jack stood up and, walking toward the old altar, dropped to his knees in front of it and prayed to his Lord. Lydia realized that Hebron was beside her, and as she looked back, she saw Elizabeth with Barael standing just inside the busted doors of the entrance. Aaron and Jeffrey were coming down the aisle toward her; all had supernaturally manifested themselves. The room was lit from the auras that surrounded the seven beings that stood waiting for Jack to finish communicating with Almighty God.

No one dared to interrupt even knowing that time was extremely short. They expected that by now, Lucifer had come to the inevitable conclusion that his army of demons had failed their assignment. And with their failure, the full impact of what was happening at an insignificant plot of ground located in the middle of the small state of Oklahoma was of the utmost importance to Almighty God.

Knowing that the significance of this charade would impact all of humanity, his rage at having been deceived so completely would be felt by the entire demonic realm. He would be coming with his greatest warriors, intent on wiping out all of God's angels, and most surely with the purpose of destroying the souls that held such significance to the Great I Am.

25

Jack raised his head, opened his eyes, and was surprised at the light that filled the area around him. Rising to his feet, he turned around and faced an unbelievable sight. Seven beings stood facing him, four of the largest most incredible creatures, dressed in long white robes, enormous scabbards hanging from their waist, and sandals on their feet.

The other three included Lydia, a young woman with auburn hair, and a young man with his head shaved clean, all emitting an aura of light that surrounded them and filled every crevice of the old sanctuary.

All were smiling at him, and Jack felt an overwhelming affection for each of them.

Aaron stepped forward and spoke first, "Jack, we are so glad you decided to join us. I think it's time for you to meet Orion. He has been with you all of your life."

Jack assumed this breathtaking creature was the leader of them. The one who must be Orion came toward him as Aaron moved aside. Jack stared up at him and knew beyond doubt that they had known each other all of his life.

"I guess I owe you one heck of an apology, and you have it. I wish I had been different. If I could change—" Jack began a litany of apologies.

He was cut short by Orion's reaction. "Don't! Looking back is not useful. Your decision today has restored me to my full strength." Turning to face the others, he said, "Now, we must ready ourselves."

Jack looked around quizzically, not understanding what they all seemed to be aware of.

Again, Aaron assumed his role of leader and quickly explained, "Jack, last night, a great battle was fought here."

"That kind of explains why I felt so frightened and on edge."

"Yes, we had to get you into the church where we could protect you with the others. We were significantly concerned that you might try to leave."

"There was no chance of that, I can assure you," Jack said with a grin on his face.

Aaron continued with his explanation of what had occurred. "Lucifer sent a legion of his demons to wipe out the four of us and capture the souls of God's children. He did not realize the importance of you four, but he was suspicious that God's mightiest warriors had been assigned the mundane task of taking care of humans. We had recently wiped out the lowly demons that had harassed all of you and that really got his attention. We have hidden ourselves here until time for the Rapture. All of the names in the Book of Life have been entered except for you. You four souls, that have been hidden here, are the last four names to be entered into the Book of Life and the key to opening the cataclysmic events that will occur. God did not want to lose you four, so all of the heavenly realms have waited for your decisions. You are the last of the four."

The words hung in the air as they stared at each other. Lydia was the first to react, "What are we supposed to do now?"

The four mighty warriors answered in unison, "Pray!"

One by one, they dropped to their knees and began to praise Almighty God. First, they lifted their individual voices, but soon, they were filled with the Holy Spirit and their voices united into one voice speaking in a tongue known to Almighty God.

The warriors were overcome from the intensity of the combined faith of their charges and lowering themselves to their knees bowed their heads and prayed with gratitude to Jehovah for allowing them to survive the previous night.

As the eight filled the small chapel with praise, Lucifer, situated on the other side of the world, was awakened to his error. Realizing he had been duped, his wrath consumed him. The echoes of his angry screams reverberated around the earth in the form of lightning and thunder like the world had never seen. He flew across the sky killing whatever crossed his path including his own demonic warriors.

Lowly demons to seasoned warriors searched frantically for hiding places wherever they could find them, drew their quivering wings in tight around their bodies, and remained silent hoping Lucifer's great wrath would wane. An eerie silence came over the surface of the earth as all living creatures held their breath and waited. There was no normal any longer. People, animals, and the creatures of the deep oceans were waiting for something to happen. And nine-tenths of the world population had no idea that an answer was theirs for the asking.

His anger spent at last, Satan stood at the top of the world and called out his legions. They arrived, hesitantly at first, afraid their leader was prepared to sacrifice them all, but his rage had modified now that he had formulated a plan in his head. He was thinking clearly, and a smile played across his face as he anticipated what was to come.

His plan was perfected down to the last detail. As he outlined it to his generals, they knew there was no way he would tolerate failure. Better to die at the hands of the heavenly angels than to face the fury of their leader. So they prepared themselves for the monumental battle ahead of them.

Deep in the bowels of earth fires roared as anvils were used to sharpen swords and spears. Generals screeched out orders and down the line the serpentlike demons raced to obey. All of purgatory was alive with constant motion, and for a while, the grateful prisoners were ignored.

And at the throne, Father and Son watched and waited.

Thick, rolling, pure white clouds began to collect high above the atmosphere, gathering larger and larger until they blocked out the sun on one side of the earth and blocked the moon from being seen during the night on the other side.

It was just past dusk at Gable Cemetery. The eight continued their praise and worship inside the chapel, oblivious to the passing of time. Remaining on their knees, they did not tire as the hours went by. So committed to praising God, time had no meaning to them.

During the stillness of night, a trumpet rang out; its deep booming sound resonated around the globe. Those who heard the magnificent notes coming from Gabriel's horn thought even the deaf must be able to hear it. The dense clouds parted as the dead in Christ rose first. Surrounded by the vivid colors of reds, yellows, golds, and blues swirling around them, they were lifted up toward the brightest of lights to the figure robed in white linen waiting with arms opened wide to welcome them home.

The four souls of Gable Cemetery, along with those who had been waiting in their graves, were lifted up in the blink of an eye. Instantly, they were followed by the souls of the living. The multitudes of believers eagerly sped upward toward the parted clouds, filled with joy and anticipation. The music coming from the cloud was beyond anything ever heard before. The voices of the heavenly choir joined with the angels of Almighty God in a song of praise for the King of Kings and Lord of Lords. His arms were outstretched in welcome, his hands still bearing the scars of the crucifixion; the scars a permanent testimony of His great love for this imperfect creature He was calling to himself.

As the last soul passed through the opening into the portals of heaven, the clouds drew together and rose higher and higher until they could no longer be seen by those left on earth.

The four mighty warriors were surprised at the timing of the greatest event in human history. They had believed their battle with Satan would be here inside these small grounds, but Michael had received his instructions from the Throne. If the unthinkable happened and even one demon had escaped to tell their master of the defeat at the hands of legions of God's warriors, then time would have run out, as the entire heavenly host waited for the last soul to return to his Creator.

26

The Rapture was over.

For those who were called on the night side of earth, there was little immediate panic, but for those who were raptured during the light of day, the aftermath was so intense the media outlets were scrambling to get footage of the carnage left in its wake. It was early, only a few minutes since the saints had been called home.

Satan was concentrating completely on the plan to destroy those who stood between him and victory over God. He had summoned every demon from throughout the countries to assist in the making of the arsenal. And without rest, they feverously worked night and day until he stood before them and said, "We are ready!" So intent on the coming victory, he had no time to oversee what was happening on earth. Nothing was allowed to interfere with his plan of revenge. He relished the image of when the battle was over and he had taken the place of God, then they would return victorious and deal with the inhabitants around the globe!

They took to the air, led by their leader, and the vast numbers of demons filled the sky until the land below was bathed in dismal darkness.

The grim face of dawn was blotted out by the evil militia approaching the central state of Oklahoma. The cemetery was completely silent as the mass drew nearer. A heavy mist had turned into a dense icy fog turning the bare branches of the blackjack trees into glistening frozen fingers reaching toward the sunless sky. A strong north wind blew southward but had no effect on the scores of demons swiftly approaching the cemetery.

Lucifer was dressed in his finest, befitting a ruler of the universe, and his appearance was without question the most beautiful of all those in creation. As the demon horde drew near the cemetery, a twittering and murmuring escaped the mouths of those on the front lines announcing their arrival. The anticipation of victory over God's angel warriors caused the legions of Satan's army to rush toward the site of battle, led by their great leader.

Suddenly, he lowered his gigantic wings, and the legions behind him followed suit. Confused by this unexpected turn of events, they eyed each other warily. Lucifer drew his sword with one hand and raising it high over his head motioned them to halt. He turned his head first in one direction, then the other, sniffing the air for a scent of angels. A look of disbelief furrowed his perfect features, and he dropped stealthily down and stood before the decrepit church.

Looking around, he listened intently but saw only the pitifully neglected burial grounds and heard only the sound of the few remaining dried leaves rustling on the blackjack trees. Rushing inside the abandoned house of worship, he bounded across the broken doors as his wrath began to grow at the emptiness of it all.

The confused mass of demons surrounded the cemetery grounds and filled the sky for hundreds of miles in all directions. They were growing agitated and began to fear this turn of events, where were the huge armies they had come prepared to overpower and slay for their master?

Satan walked out of the tiny church, his enormous wings spread out from his body as screams of anger exploded from his throat. The façade of his perfect countenance began to break apart and fall away, revealing his true self. The evil grotesque creature that remained mirrored a clear image of his heart. Fear erupted among the demons as they scattered from the cemetery grounds to escape the grasp of their leader.

As he continued his frenzied tirade, he paid no heed that his terrified warriors had fled from his presence, and he was left alone in front of the small empty decaying church.

A light, brighter than the sun, appeared over him and remained as he froze, paralyzed in fear. He shuddered violently as a voice came down from heaven and addressed him.

"I am the Great I Am. You are too late, Lucifer. The souls of my faithful are safely here with me. You have lost. The Trinity is united for the first time since the Day of Pentecost. You will be given seven years to reign upon the earth to fulfill the prophecy of my word. At the end of the seven years, I will return, and at that time, you will feel my wrath!"

The voice was gone, as well as the blinding light, leaving only emptiness and darkness in its wake. Complete silence hung over the land until it was broken by the anguished screams of Lucifer and the terrified shrieks of his demons as they raced to get further away from their infuriated master.

For I am convinced that neither death, nor life, neither angels, nor demons, neither the present, nor the future, nor any powers, neither height, nor depth, nor anything else in all creation, will be able to separate us from the love of God that is in Christ Jesus, our Lord.

—Romans 8:38–39

Epilogue

Twenty-eight years before the Rapture, a baby was born in Italy only a few miles from the ecclesiastical Vatican City. His mother was a devoted, faithful follower of Lucifer.

She was the high priestess of a coven consisting of thirteen witches and warlocks. They were an unusual group, highly educated, heads of businesses, financial institutions, a select few were gifted with talent for performing, and they dwelled among the most famous of all the arts. They controlled vast amounts of wealth scattered across the globe. Their influence covered the entertainment industries, oil and gas conglomerates, and the top echelon of technology companies.

They spread their tentacles of evil over the continents like a massive spider web, and they were rewarded well by the creature they worshipped and to whom they dedicated their lives.

Three days after the birth, the exceptionally beautiful and healthy baby boy was offered up, dedicated to a lifetime of service, to Lucifer. Once the greatest angel in heaven, Lucifer recognized the special attributes of this exceptional child and excitedly accepted the baby boy as his adopted son.

No one knew who was the father of this extraordinary child, but there were whispers that strange gatherings had occurred in the hours of deepest night when an enormous black bird had been seen as it circled above her estate and was seen leaving in the early hours of dawn.

Lucifer put a hedge of protection around the child and assigned his most faithful followers to guard him all the days of his life. To impress upon them the importance of this male child, he marked him with three numbers, 666.

He was protected and watched over as he grew to adulthood. He attended the finest schools, spoke a multitude of languages, and charmed all those with whom he came into contact, all in preparation for the time when he would be brought forth to rule the world.

The Antichrist was on the earth, secluded from the eyes of the world as he prepared for his role, and his time was almost at hand. He was ready.

The hours after "the Rapture" brought enormous chaos around the earth. Planes dropped from the sky as pilot's seats were suddenly vacated; trucks and cars created huge traffic pileups along miles of interstates and byways, as empty vehicles plowed through streets and highways leaving piles of wreckage and countless deaths in their paths.

Surgeons disappeared in an instant during harrowing surgeries, firemen were unaccounted for in the middle of fires that grew and turned whole neighborhoods and entire blocks of suburban cities into infernos.

Pastors left empty pulpits for surprised congregations, pews were vacated in some churches while others barely noticed the select few who were missing. The remaining pastors, elders, and deacons did their best to quiet and give comfort to their terrified members who flocked to churches in search of answers. They were as confused and frightened as the ones they counseled, as they tried to explain the unexplainable.

The Holy Spirit had left. His presence no longer held in check the darkest desires of those remaining, and without His influence, evil grew across the land like a dissolute growing cancer.

The "good people" were shattered, frightened almost to death, as they searched for some understanding of the cataclysmic events that broke out across the earth. They always assumed they were leading decent lives, were pillars in their communities, donated their time and money to charities and attended church on special holidays; surely, they had been good enough to get them a ticket into heaven when their time came. Why would they have need of God when they were perfectly capable of leading their lives without interference?

Heads of state, generals, policy makers, the movers and shakers of the political world, many were gone in one second of earth time, as governments fell apart like dominoes swept off a table. International stock markets crashed in frenetic confusion. Communication giants collapsed and the surviving population became isolated in their individual worlds.

There was no place to escape, no security, and no safety anywhere. The planet reeled as earthquakes erupted across the globe. Solar storms fired around the sun causing fierce storms and massive tornadoes to sweep across the earth leaving death and destruction in their wake. The death tolls mounted to unfathomable numbers until mass graves were dug and filled over and over.

The life-enhancing miracles that had functioned for so long without being noticed, now failed. Nothing continued to work as it had before the Rapture. Utility grids were destroyed as the normal chain of actions were destroyed, water taps went dry, electricity switches no longer responded, furnaces stopped flowing with warmth, nothing worked any longer. Grocery stores were left with empty shelves after looters came and left. Food, any kind of food, was mostly unavailable, and deaths from starvation rose dramatically.

Every day became filled with unimaginable fear as the inhabitants left behind struggled to survive a living nightmare. Minds were lost, families turned on each other for a crust of bread, murders increased by the tens of thousands, suicides became commonplace.

And in the midst of this overwhelming misery, a group rose up out of the pandemonium with a charismatic leader at its helm. He was barely over thirty, handsome, with slightly graying hair at his temples, tall and stately, his voice deep and calming as he promised all of the surviving inhabitants, he would save them and bring reconciliation back to the planet. He promised peace instead of chaos, order instead of turmoil, and life instead of death.

He had a plan, a great plan, to bring all countries under a one world government, a universal world kingdom with its capitol in Jerusalem, one religion that all people would be welcomed into, ruled by a worshipped leader. And at his right hand would stand a man who would present himself as a holy pope to all, not just to surviving Catholics.

The unholy trinity would at last be in place. Satan, the Antichrist, and the False Prophet prepared to rule a dying world.

Satan's plan, formed in the aftermath of his humiliating defeat, became reality.

One government, one religion, one god, to be worshipped by all.

One god, who carried the mark of the beast, three numbers hidden on his body.

666

Also by Robbie Lamberson:

My Sarah

The Queen of Cuss and Her Redheaded Treasure

About the Author

Robbie Lamberson is a widow, mother, grandmother, great-grand-mother, author, Christian speaker, cancer survivor, and lover of life. She has lived a life filled with travel and exciting adventures, which she chronicled in her previous novel, *The Queen of Cuss and Her Redheaded Treasure.* She is working on her fourth novel, speaking at women's retreats, organizations, and churches. Robbie donates time to fundraising for her favorite nonprofit and makes time for exercising and line dancing. She currently lives in Norman, Oklahoma, and shares her home with two pugs, referred to as "the girls".

CPSIA information can be obtained
at www.ICGtesting.com
Printed in the USA
FFOW02n1123101217
43988575-43150FF

9 781641 148696